Hemlock

Joyce Doré

Hemlock

Joyce Doré

Braiswick

Braiswick at B y Design
111 High Road East,
Felixstowe, Suffolk IP11 9PS

ISBN 1 898030 87 1

British Library Cataloguing in Publication Data
available.

Cover design by Eileen Aldous

Printed by Lightning Source
Braiswick is an imprint of Catherine Aldous Design Ltd

Glossary

Alesund: Boudica's homeland.

Betulanter: Wise woman at Dere well.

Boudica (Boudicca): Queen of the Iceni.

Camulodunum: Colchester.

Caradoc: Son of Cunobelinus.

Caratacus: Romanised version of Caradoc.

Cavantina: Eldest daughter of Boudica and Prasutagus.

Ceridwen: their younger daughter.

Celts: The nation of people covering most of Europe including the British islands.

Cunobelinus: King of Camulodunum, Shakespeare's Cymbeline.

Druids: High priests of the Celts, whose centre was on the island of Mona, now know as Anglesey.

Fililpenda: Bereaved mother at Dere Well.

Garian: Headman of the Iceni settlement.

Gariannonum: Burgh castle.

Icenorum Venta: Prasutagus' kingdom, which covered most of East Anglia.

Julius Classicus: Roman officer and spy, Boudica's lover.

Leofing: Chief druid.

Marius Sextus: Boudica's other lover.

Nero: Roman emperor.

Prasutagus: King of the Iceni, Druid chief and husband of Boudica.

Ratae Coriatnorum: Leicester.

Suetonus Paulinus: Roman Governor General of Britain.

Shar: Bodyguard to Prasutagus.

Trinovantes: Tribes of Sussex and Essex.

Togodumnus: Son of Cunoblinus, killed by the Romans.

Uritcor: Head man at the flint mines

Chapter 1

The summer evening felt warm as Victoria drove the seven miles towards Julia's home in Wisbech; the new moon hung as a silver sickle in the early evening, and stars gleamed like precious jewels in the darkening sky. The feathers of gold and ruby from the setting sun reflected on the wisps of clouds and from there into her eyes, making her frown in an attempt to cut down the glare. The heat of the day had made the tar on the road sticky and Victoria wondered if fog would form once the sun had set.

For the moment, the oncoming darkness created soft shadows among the trees and shrubs in orchards and gardens, and the road ahead was almost deserted.

Victoria's concentration wavered for a few seconds as she considered the coming evening's entertainment. Apart from Steve and Julia Compton, her hosts, she would not know anyone else at the party and she felt a tremor of indecision trickle through her resolve. They had asked her to come as a special favour, to meet the new neighbours and acquaintances they had made since they had moved to Wisbech.

There were already several cars parked alongside the road as she pulled in behind some that were rather large and expensive looking. Victoria's confidence wavered. She began to wonder if she really should have come. However she found that the housewarming party to which she had been invited, was good-natured and friendly.

Careful to whom she spoke, not wanting to be mistaken for someone hunting for a partner, she was at pains not to intrude on any conversation that she thought might be private, but no one seemed at all concerned that she was alone. They asked Victoria to comment on the topics that they were discussing, treating her as a companion with the conversation flowing smoothly and sociably. The

1

pleasant crowd encouraged Victoria to feel part of their lives too when they asked her to a barbecue the following week.

Victoria felt as though she was coming to life again for the first time after being buried in deep apathy for many years. She had only agreed to come to Julia's party as long as there was no attempt to pair her off with a man.

A feeling of peace stole over her, and the impression of happiness made her smile as she chatted to the other guests, and began to unwind.

Walking along the patio path with a glass of ruby wine in her hand, a tremor of excitement ran through her body like a minor earthquake causing her hand to shake and making the wine slop over the rim of her glass. Steadying herself again, Victoria stepped down into the scented garden.

Finding a comfortable bench, she sat and looked back at the carefree partygoers as they twisted to an old Beatles record, the way they had done as teenagers with little to worry about except acne!

Victoria took a deep, refreshing breath then sipping the rich fruity wine, she thought about the years she had spent trying to make sense of the marriage that had broken her heart and isolated her from all of her friends except Julia.

Relaxed, she was able to review the past without rancour. This invitation had been the first that she had accepted since her acrimonious divorce from James.

Now she was free, free of the constant nagging worry about where he was and who he was with, free from eking out enough money to pay for the necessities of living and wondering if he had raided the housekeeping money again.

For many years Victoria had been kept busy caring for her two sons and keeping the home clean and tidy. Cash had been too short to join any clubs where she could meet other Navy wives and mothers. The bus fares into town made a hole in the meagre amount of money that James gave her. Once Victoria had paid all the running costs of managing the home, there was precious little left over for food let alone luxuries.

During her marriage, Victoria had become several pounds under weight, but lately the rounded curves that had been hers when she was younger, had returned.

Her hair that had become limp and dull within a short time of marrying James was gradually growing back to the cloud of spun gold with copper undertones.

Once more Victoria felt proud to be a woman and was taking an interest in fashionable clothes again. Her job as officer in charge of the small post office in a village on the outskirts of King's Lynn paid enough for her to buy a cottage and indulge herself with driving lessons. Eventually she had been able to purchase her Mini, that was the colour of a ripe tomato.

Her spare time was usually spent working in the large country garden that came with the cottage, which had once housed the weavers and spinners of the wool sheared from the local sheep. It had been a thriving industry until James Hargreaves had invented the Spinning Jenny in 1767 for spinning cotton, and Sir Richard Arkwright had improved upon it in 1775, enabling the machines to spin and weave wool, taking all the cottagers' work away from them.

When the bales of wool were sent to the mills far away in Nottingham, the weavers had either died out or moved to where there was employment for them, rather than starve to death.

Victoria had been told of a child, a young girl who had disappeared when food became very scarce in the cottage in the early 1800's. With two other, younger children to feed as well as himself and his wife, the father had been at his wits' end to know how to feed them.

The growing young girl whom they had called Grace, ate the most food in the little household. When it was gossiped about that she had gone to live with relatives and was seen no more, no one had felt any need to ask more questions. Many years later her remains had been found when a new tenant moved in the cottage and the beaten earth floor had been replaced with cement.

Grace's father admitted that he had hung her by her neck from the oak beam in the tiny back bedroom so that he could carry on feeding the rest of his pathetic family.

As she toiled in the garden Victoria always thought of that deprived youngster and felt no fear of the child's spirit when she slept in the little back room that overlooked the rear garden, rather than sleep in the large front one that faced the lane, for it was in that room that she always felt a chill.

Chapter 2

The atmosphere in Julia's garden was peaceful, sweet and pure, a reflection of her present life, Victoria thought. She wished for nothing more and breathed it in gratefully.

The memory of the aunt who had adopted her and had turned her out onto the streets at the impressionable age of sixteen, with the venomous declaration that still rang in her ears, "Get out! I don't want you here. You're nothing but trouble, just like your father…and he gave you away because he didn't want you either!" resurfaced in her head but harsh words no longer tortured her. She felt that her father, who had died long ago, had allowed her Aunt Bessy to adopt her when Victoria's mother had died, in the belief that his little daughter was going to a better home.

Victoria had sat on a park bench that evening, wondering where she could sleep, and that was when Lucy, a happy extrovert, who worked in the same office as she did, made herself known. They became firm friends and Lucy had taken Victoria to stay with old Miss Clarissa Askew.

For a few brief years, life had been perfect for Victoria. Clarissa Askew seemed to know everything about her and had shown her more love and kindness than she would ever encounter again.

The elderly lady had the reputation of being slightly mad and rather weird with odd friends. It had transpired that far from being mad she was very sane. Her only claim to being weird was that she was a medium and held a psychic development circle once a week.

When she was eighteen years old, Miss Askew had introduced Victoria to the psychic circle and she had proved to be an adept medium too.

Then James had waltzed into her life at the wedding of Julia, the sister of another office friend, and Steve Compton, Julia's new husband.

James had swept her into his arms and around the ballroom making her heart beat to a rhythm that she had never known before.

He was far too handsome in his naval uniform. The image of his dark, sombre features had stayed with her wherever she went, and his sardonic attitude had even haunted her dreams.

Victoria had eventually agreed to marry him after he had repeatedly insisted that she became his wife. Miss Askew had made it plain that she did not like Victoria's choice of husband and during the marriage ceremony had cast rueful glances at James dressed in his smart Naval uniform, but she had kept her counsel.

Victoria's dreams had become nightmares when the new typist Jean, had glanced out of the office window and declared, "There goes Jimmy, my boyfriend!"

Out of curiosity, Victoria had looked to discover who the lucky young man might be. The jaunty stepping young man was none other than James, her husband. They had been married only six months.

Victoria remembered that first time when James had betrayed her with wistful melancholy. He had denied any association with Jean, the argument had been bitter, with James storming out of the neat little home that they shared.

When James had returned he was moody and morose, sulking as if the row had been all Victoria's fault, and for the sake of peace she had said no more. James had then become more attentive to her and took her to the mess parties at the Naval base that were being held at Christmas.

Victoria had saved for many weeks from her meagre housekeeping money that James had given her, suspecting that she might be pregnant and would need to buy new baby clothes. When this had proven to be a false alarm she spent the money on a new turquoise, oyster satin dress, for a mess party.

6

As she danced with James and several of his friends, her happiness was complete. James had bought her numerous glasses of wine, and never having had much cash to spare for such luxuries at home, the unaccustomed alcohol made her very light headed. The evening passed in a flash.

When it was time to go home, James had offered a lift to Sally, a friend's wife. He explained that Fergus, Sally's husband, was away on a Naval exercise in the Mediterranean Sea. He couldn't leave the poor "sea widow" to find her own way home could he, James had reasoned.

"I'll drop you off first Vicki, then I'll take Sally home. She lives quite far along the London road so don't wait up. I'll be back as soon as I can." Without any suspicion, Victoria had fallen into bed in a slightly drunken stupor.

James's return had been noiseless. Victoria had neither heard nor felt him come to bed. Next morning he was sympathetic about her headache and fussed over her before he returned to his ship.

Victoria felt that there was something amiss but could not place the imperfection. Was James being too kind? Was that bizarre smile on his face hiding something, she wondered?

When he came home that evening, all Victoria's suspicions were forgotten as once again, James held her in his arms and whispered endearments, and he continued to pay her compliments, gaining her unreserved trust and love again.

Some months later, Victoria realised that she was pregnant, and her contentment was complete. The baby would cement their relationship forever, or so she had thought.

Her second baby was the fulfilment of her existence; Victoria felt that her life was now perfect, except that Peter seemed to be acutely jealous of his baby brother, Clive.

Victoria had tried to humour the little boy, but he seemed to resent her even bathing him with Clive. Nothing would bring a smile to the child's face and he would push her away when she tried to cuddle him.

Victoria found this behaviour difficult to understand, because Peter had been such a jolly, mischievous child before the birth of Clive.

James's frequent absences were excused as being Duty Watch Officer, and Victoria had no reason to disbelieve him until a woman telephoned and asked for her darling Jimmy!

Stunned, Victoria called her husband to the telephone to tell him that, "Darling, wants him to come as soon as he can."

Again the recriminations, and the sulking little boy act, but this time Victoria decided that enough was enough and asked James to leave.

"I've nowhere to go!" he blurted out. "You can't turn me out just like that!" His anger made his deep blue eyes turn a muddy grey, and there was menace in his stance. It seemed as if his groping, outstretched hands were ready to strangle her, and Victoria suddenly felt seriously afraid. Icy fingers of realisation tore away the blinkers of naiveté. How could she have been so stupid? Instinctively she knew her life was in deadly danger. James was unstable. He would never change and become a reliable adult.

When James thought she was not listening or watching, he had verbally abused the children and found fault with them, and flicked his fingers about their ears. This, Victoria realised, had revealed his jealousy of the children and explained little Peter's odd behaviour.

There had been the aggressive arguments when she had called him to task. James had whined, asserting that it was the children's fault. He could never accept that he was in the wrong.

Then of course there was always his compulsion to have affairs with other women, yet he expected her to stay conscientiously at home.

It was obvious that there were two characters lurking in the person that she believed to be her husband. One was the kind caring person who loved her and whom she loved in return, and this other creature who would stop at nothing to gain his own ends. Yet at no time had she been aware of this flaw in his personality during their whirlwind courtship. It had seemed then that James was nothing less than a normal kind and caring man.

That was long ago. The bitter truth had emerged eventually, and by the time the divorce was made absolute, she was so resentful and confused, she was unable to talk to anyone she did not know intimately. This was particularly so with men.

Chapter 3

Looking over her shoulder and taking stock of the cheerful laughter, and the light-hearted attitude of Julia's friends, Victoria decided from that moment, she would never again allow her ex-husband to sour her spirit. She was going to enjoy every minute of her life. There was a mature artists' class in King's Lynn and a psychic circle that she could join.

Victoria knew from her experience of the circle that Clarissa had run, that she would need to approach the circle leader for entrance. Yes, she decided, the time for depression and loneliness was over! She would make new friends and enjoy herself again.

Julia had been watching Victoria from the concealment of the shrubbery. She could see that her young friend was meditating on the past and was pleased to note the resolve forming on Victoria's attractive features. She called out to her and interrupted her friend's musing. "Come on Victoria! It's no time for pondering over that object called James. No one is more sorry than I that you two had to meet at my wedding. So, no more gloomy weekends alone for you my young friend." With that Julia led her to where the food and drink were being served.

Victoria laughed joyously at Julia's ploy to get her past the horror of being married to James. Her heart was still sore and she wondered how she had come to be so easily misled by him. Why had she been so infatuated with James? It was as if he had some strange power over her!

The party came to its natural end at one in the morning. Julia, with some lingering guests, had waved good-bye to Victoria. "Take the second turning on the left, Victoria," Julia had said, "and you will be on the A47 to King's Lynn. You can't miss it."

The lights from the windows and open door had sent shafts of golden paths across the dark lawns lighting her way to the little car standing at the kerb.

Victoria turned, laughing, as she waved good-bye, promising to visit them again for the barbecue the following week. The car started at the first turn of the key, and letting in the clutch, carefully she manoeuvred the Mini out of the line of cars still parked there, and onto the main road, keeping Julia's instructions firmly in her mind.

Most of the houses that she passed were in darkness though some, like Julia's, had curtains wide open to spill the yellow lamplight out into the night and display the cheerful ambience of homes with their occupants still enjoying the weekend break.

The thrill of the evening's happiness lingered as she drove along the street, watching for the second turning. When she reached it, the road seemed much narrower than Victoria expected it to be and the streetlights seemed dimmer.

That's odd, she thought, perhaps it's a short cut. The main road can't be far away. However, the road soon petered down to a restricted lane, with no lamplight at all, and ditches full of water had replaced the paths.

The euphoria that she felt earlier gradually melted away, to be replaced by a feeling of progressive foreboding, and her heart sank when she realised that she was hopelessly lost. "Oh, for the bright lights of King's Lynn," she whispered forlornly to herself.

The night had turned cheerless, and the once scintillating stars were now hidden behind the gathering clouds and vapour rising from the midnight darkened fields.

She stopped the little car, and got out to have a better view of her surroundings. The low-slung Mini did not permit her to see over the top of the dike bank when she sat at the wheel.

When Victoria's feet touched the asphalt road, she stood in the unearthly atmosphere and glanced about, feeling so uncertain of her surroundings that, she wished that she had taken up Julia's offer of a bed and stayed in Wisbech.

The night air had begun to feel dank; it seemed to cling to her hair and felt like cloying spider's webs on her face. There was only a slight breath of wind to stir the sentinel reeds that grew along the water's edge.

Wraiths of mist curled up from the moist, peat scented, dark earth, uncaring in its meandering spiral upwards, roving and drifting where it would …and silence. "I don't need this," Victoria muttered into the eerie atmosphere. She heaved a sigh of resignation, her breath slightly misting the cool night air.

The headlights of her car showed dead straight, empty road, with ditches on both sides, making it impracticable to turn and go back the way that she had come. She stood listening for a few moments more, but the only sound to reach her ears was the faint tinkling of water as it drained from the fenland into the ditch.

Shaking her head in confusion, Victoria opened the car door again and eased herself back into the seat. She decided that there was nothing for it but to continue on this road to its end, then perhaps with some luck there would be a signpost giving directions to King's Lynn.

A feeling of lassitude began to creep over her. She would be glad to close her eyes and sleep. Fortunately it was Sunday and she could rest as long as she wanted once she reached home. Slowly, she set off again, keeping a watchful eye open for any sign of habitation or a crossroad.

Half an hour later the night seemed even more dismal than before, and the light breeze that had stirred the reed bed was stilled. The mist had become a curtain of thick haze, shifting and dancing. Twinges of panic formed a tight knot in Victoria's throat. She slowed the car, gently easing her foot onto the brake ready to stop as a swirling cloud of fog, more solid than the rest, started to gain contours and form.

The tremors of fear in the pit of her stomach were making her feel light headed and queasy. The desire to put her foot down hard on the accelerator to get the widest distance between her and whatever it was that happening here was overwhelming, but Victoria eased the car to a standstill once again.

This isn't happening, she thought. But an indistinct phantom gradually appeared in front of her and slowly took the silhouette of a tall, well-built woman. In the headlight, her hair hung pale and loose about her shoulders, writhing and coiling as if it had a life of its own.

Switching off the engine, tight lipped, Victoria got out of the car even though dread clawed at her heart making it difficult for her to breathe. She felt duty-bound to make certain it was not someone who needed help.

The apparition solidified, turned and looked at Victoria with eyes that were sad and pleading. The right arm was so badly broken that the bone showed through the torn skin and the useless hand hung down slackly.

In a heart-rending and inquiring manner, the spirit held out the broken arm to Victoria as if to say, "Look at me. Look at what they did to me!"

The gossamer thin, white robe that the phantom wore was dirty and slashed to ribbons. She beckoned with her left hand, and Victoria, drawn on by powers beyond her own, was dragged towards this restless spirit.

It smiled at her like an endearing loving friend who was about to impart an intimate secret as it placed its good left hand on her right shoulder. Victoria was powerless, unable to move a muscle and escape this nightmare. Her throat was closed and dry, and her jaws were clamped so tightly shut, her breathing almost stopped.

She stood staring in amazement and wonder, not daring to move in case this tableau should disappear.

Then, Victoria's overwhelming desire to learn more, brushed aside all fear and allowed herself to enter the waiting arms.

The scales of blindness to the etheric world had been partially wiped from her eyes by Clarissa Askew. Her appetite for more enlightenment had not been blunted by her disastrous marriage, nor had her exuberance for life. They had only been suppressed until now. Now the dam that had been breached at Julia's party was in full flood. Victoria no longer shivered with panic, but excitement!

The feeling of exhilaration overcame any vestige of remaining dread, and Victoria was determined not to permit any tiny trickle of anxiety to deny her this wonderful chance of experiencing contact with what was obviously, a spirit who so desperately needed respite.

Chapter 4

Slowly, as the encounter proceeded, Victoria felt uninhibited as she was enfolded in an embrace by the spectre and became part of this demented entity. She was being invited to experience something it was trying to convey to her. The anticipation of the unknown, coursed through her veins like molten lead. A chance like this came only once in a lifetime, if then, and this opportunity was not to be wasted on nervous dithering. Resolve bit like a hunting terrier with its teeth sunk deep into a rat. It would not let go until it had been appeased.

Suddenly she was no longer on a deserted road in the middle of the Fens. Instead Victoria found herself in a clearing in the middle of a dark wood. Only the stars gave light to many people who were gathered.

Looking about, she wondered why no campfires had been lit. Then Victoria picked up on the fear permeating the atmosphere. She realised that these people were desperate fugitives, hiding from something or someone.

The flicker of flames would have beckoned anyone searching for them, and the tell-tale sweet smell of the wood smoke drifting on the night air would surely have led anyone to the fire from whence it came. No smoke without fire was certainly a true axiom.

People lay slumped and weary in twos and threes, their heads resting anywhere there was something to act as a cushion. Some had their heads on the laps of a comrade, others on a mossy knoll. Their exhaustion was complete. The dell was as silent as the grave. No word was uttered, and no sound broke the stillness of the night. Heavy earth scents mingled with the sweat of terror, hung motionless in the gloom.

Victoria became aware of a woman propped up against the bole of a vast, gnarled oak. She was trying to comfort a slim, fair-haired, young girl who was trembling in her arms.

Abruptly the quiet of the forest was shattered! Everyone leapt to their feet, swords in hand. The fugitives were ambushed and out numbered by dozens of screaming soldiers.

The fearsome warriors appeared to be dressed in dark kilts and held bronze shields that echoed with the sound of a death sentence as they rattled their spears and swords against them. The wearied party had come to their feet painfully and attempted to fight back bravely, but their fatigue let them down and they were easily quelled.

Some of the uniformed soldiers ignited rush lights, giving the scene an unearthly ambience. Distorted, inky black shadows of the fighters danced and bounced from the gigantic tree trunks like mad cavorting demons. Screams of anguish echoed and reverberated from the massive oaks as the wounded and dying were brutally slaughtered.

Never had Victoria seen and heard of such a conflict between even the most hated of enemies. As it was splashed over the clearing like a charnel house, the smell of blood made her feel sick. She felt as if her bones would melt. She was certain that this battle had taken place centuries before and all that she was seeing was a replay especially for her benefit, displayed by the ghost who was her mentor.

Victoria realised that the woman who had met her, was in fact her guide and now she had taken her place in the tableau. She glanced up hastily to where two men stood apart from the fray. One was a Roman general. The other was dressed in the Roman fashion of white toga and cloak, his face partially hidden in the darkness. In the gloom the woman had managed to discern the features of a face that she had once adored. It was Julius, Julius Classicus!

Now Victoria realised that her guide and mentor was sharing her thoughts, her feelings and her life when she had been alive at this time. She felt the woman's heart sink, knowing now that it was Julius, her lover, who had betrayed them to the enemy. She tried to scream, "Traitor!" but a swift blow to the back of her head from the hilt of a soldier's sword, sent her to her knees making her dizzy and see flashing lights. Still she struggled to her feet from the mossy ground, and flew at the opponent who had attacked her.

Then the girl, whom the woman had been nursing, was now defending her back, but the child too was brutally punched to the ground by a man whose fists were covered with gore. His snarling face was a mask of bestiality as he drooled at the prospect of destroying such a beautiful young girl, and his intentions became obvious when he raised his kilt. He threw the child to the ground and fell upon her.

Gradually the clamour of the conflict was stilled. Dragged by her hair, the woman was brought to where the Governor General of the Roman army, Suetonius Paulinus stood alone. His treacherous companion had slunk quietly off into the dense woods, taking the path that ran beside the waterfall and stream.

Suetonius had travelled by forced march for days, not sparing man or beast. Word had reached him in the western regions of Anglesey in Mona, of an enlightened school of learning. Nero had commanded him to destroy all evidence of it considering it a hot bed of insurrection, teaching young people to think and ask questions.

The commanders sent to repel the Iceni uprising had refused. They were mortally afraid of her and her rag-tag army of common serfs and their families. Suetonius had found very little to compensate for the long trek across the hills and dales of Britain when he had stormed the great stone buildings, sacred to the Druids as their halls of law and wisdom.

Most of the inhabitants had escaped by sea in the tiny coracles to a large green island. All their knowledge was stored in their heads. They were known never to write anything down. Everything had to be learned and remembered in the twenty years of an acolyte's tuition. To make certain that their minds did not wander away from their lessons, the young people were not allowed to journey home in all of that time.

Suetonius decapitated every Druid who could be caught, be they young acolytes or old tutors. Their heads were pierced by long wooden pikes and placed for all to see, around the wrecked walls of the gracious buildings.

Those who had escaped by paddling their hide and wattle coracles as fast as they could on the out going tide, were washed up against the shores of their new island home, their fortunes and future, unknown.

Suetonius, insane with anger at the deceit of the falsehood, glared at the two women, his bloodshot eyes rimmed with the grit and mud of sleepless nights. "My orders are to take you alive if possible. If not, I am to take your head as evidence of your death and those of your daughters to my lord Nero." Then he looked at the rest of his captives. "Finish the men off," he barked. "The women you can use, but be quick about it, and I want these two out of the area before dawn. And take careful note of this." Suetonius had lowered his voice and those men who had served with him for some years, knew that he was ramming home a message that they dare not forget. " I want these two women guarded with your lives. If they escape, then those responsible will be crucified, gutted and then used for target practice. Do you understand?" He waited while they absorbed this order, and then continued, "Any Druid or their supporter found anywhere near them, are to have their tongues cut out and their heads mounted on a pole like those at their precious house of learning. Then he nodded his head, indicating he had finished giving his commands.

Still dazed from the blow that she had received from the sword hilt, the woman staggered to her feet. "How brave the Roman General is with women and children," she mocked him.

"Any other woman and child, yes, but not with you my Lady Queen Boudica. All Rome knows what murderous havoc you have caused in Britain, and Nero has been asked questions in the Senate as to what he intends to do with you when captured," Suetonius replied. Spittle from his cruel mouth sprayed everyone who was within an arm's reach.

"Nero plans to display you in the arena as the main attraction," he taunted, an ugly grimace displaying his rotten uneven teeth, and then looked about, his eyes searching the shadows. "I was told that you had two daughters. Where is the other?"

The furious sparks of pure hatred in her eyes should have warned Suetonius of the danger that he was in. Boudica was onto him with her teeth bared and the claws on her hands, aimed at his throat. "Your brave men took turns raping them when my oldest daughter, Cavatina, and her young sister, Ceridwen, were playing in a stream. Those men stole my children's gold torques as they assaulted them, so they *knew* that they were violating princesses." She was shaking him by his shoulders as if he were a weak aspen leaf fluttering in the wind, Suetonius was held helpless by Boudica's iron grip, unable to free himself from her maternal rage that held all watching, in deep thrall.

Boudica's face was distorted. Her teeth exposed like a wild animal and her eyes flattened into slits of sheer loathing, as a savage howl of rage escaped her. "Ceridwen brought her older sister, Cavatina, home demented. I sent Cavatina to be healed by some friendly priests. She is still with them. Go and find her if you still have the courage!" she screamed at him.

Chapter 5

Boudica bared her teeth even wider and sunk them deep into Suetonius's throat by his jugular vein. When she was torn away from her prey, her teeth and mouth were red with his gore. Suetonius's face was now the colour of the ripe sloes that grew in profusion along the hedgerows in autumn.

The shock at the effrontery he had just endured from this Iceni bitch had contorted his face. To Boudica it seemed as if Suetonius's face now looked like Loki, the corrupt dark spirit responsible for the death of Balder, the beloved son of Odin and Frigg, the god and goddess of Boudica's homeland.

The silence in the clearing was awful as the Roman General responsible for the control of the British colony, took a deep, shuddering breath.

His piercing, slate grey eyes became concentrated and fixed on Boudica. Slowly he wiped the gore from his face and neck with a filthy, sweaty rag. Then he hit Boudica across the face with the back of his hand, so viciously that her head was thrown back with the force of the blow. Her cheekbone shattered, making her left eye bulge from its socket. Boudica was once more thrust to the ground, her nose broken and bloody. This time her stunned brain refused to function well enough to allow her to rise to her feet and confront her tormentor yet again.

A protruding rock had dazed her even further than the blow, and before she could recover, Governor General Suetonius Paulinus picked up another rock. Gritting his teeth, he smashed it down on her right hand with all his might, while she was still prone on the ground.

Globules of sweat stood out on Suetonius's face. He was gasping as he bent over to grip her bruised and bloodied arm between the elbow and the wrist, in both hands.

He lifted the arm that he had seized, high above his head and brought it crashing down, shattering it over the edge of a shield. Suetonius let out a long, throbbing sob of air, his anger appeased.

Boudica's arm had snapped like a dry stick, so that the bone sprang through the white flesh of her inner arm, sending her blood spurting over Suetonius. "That should stop you and anyone else, who would carry a spear against Rome," he grated through his thin purple lips.

The shock of the pain sent Boudica plummeting down into oblivion and she slumped to her haunches once again. This time the cold night of unconsciousness that flooded her brain, stayed with her, sparing her further agony as she sank to the ground in a dead faint. The mutilation of her fighting arm was the least she should have expected.

Runaway slaves were crippled by having their hamstrings cut so that they could not even walk. They would certainly never run again, and anyone who mutinied against Rome had their fighting arm broken as a matter of course.

Boudica was only dimly aware that two rough litters had been made from a wattle fence to carry her daughter and her, not so much to spare them the gruelling journey, but to speed up the pace of the company of travellers as they made their way through the countryside. They would travel to the nearest chariot where they would then be transported to the jetty at the burnt out town of Camulodunum.

Hazily consciousness returned to Boudica's brain once more as the party jolted along the trail. Not knowing Suetonius's plans, she realised that she needed to remain watchful during the long and arduous journey. It was as much as she could do but it was essential for her to know where they were headed. Still she harboured hopes of a rescue from those Iceni warriors who had escaped the ambush.

21

These hopes were blunted when Suetonius approached with a soldier who carried a hank of thick grass plaited rope. Suetonius had decided to ensure that his prisoners would never escape him and commanded the soldier to bind Boudica tightly about the arms and shoulders. For the first time in her entire life Boudica was afraid.

Terror tore at her heart. She screamed for help from anyone within earshot who would or could assist her, but her screams were in vain. There was no one alive to listen to her plea. Any mortal who could be of assistance was Roman, and the Romans wished her dead. It was a futile act that wounded her throat and made her loosened teeth ache almost as much as her broken right arm.

Her thudding heart weighed as heavy as lead when she realised she would never escape the clutches of this man and the Roman Empire. From now on, she was a helpless captive of her most hated enemy, Nero.

Suetonius permitted no stopping for water or rest. They travelled by night as well as by day, ever eastwards. Boudica wondered if they were headed towards Camulodunum in East Anglia. If so then she would find no friends to help her to escape her abductors anywhere there. She had ransacked the community and burned every Roman occupied villa to ashes. Blood had run in the gutters of the streets, like rain in a winter storm.

The jolting and swaying of the stretcher brought her half way back to her senses. She realised that she had allowed her wits to dull and had fallen into a sleep that could harbour death.

Her mind wasn't working properly. When she tried to move her badly shattered right arm, she was reminded ferociously of her plight as splinters of searing agony lanced around her brain.

Lurid dreams had tortured her whilst she had dozed. They returned now as she lay trying to gather her wits about her. It seemed as though she had been trying to escape something or someone evil. She had been running, holding Ceridwen's hand. The evil had chased after them through barren lands, mountains and rocks where the sleeping gods trembled.

It was the nightmare that had awakened her and she thought that she had shrieked for help but no one was paying her any heed. Anyway it was useless to expect anyone to help now. To give aid to her and her daughter Ceridwen, would spell torture and death for any helper.

Her thoughts turned to the welfare of Ceridwen. Where was she? Had the Romans hurt her? These were the frightening images that plagued her brain. Boudica tried to lift her head up so that she could see the rest of the procession, but the path seemed to be narrower than the usual Roman road. It was bordered by foliage still clinging to the dripping wet, autumn branches. With her swollen and blackened half-closed eyes, she could barely see beyond the litter upon which she lay.

Eventually the convoy stopped to allow Ceridwen and Boudica to be transferred to the chariot that was to take them on the rest of the journey to the waiting boat. Boudica looked around for an opportunity to make a break for freedom, but the restraining rope and Suetonius's warning of what would happen to any soldier who neglected his duty or was lazy and allowed the prisoners any respite, made flight impossible.

After being pushed and brutally mauled by the soldiers who pretended to assist them into the chariot, Ceridwen and Boudica attempted to find some ease in each other's arms. The hard wooden bed of the cart, more used to carrying farm crops, offered little comfort. They were now together and for that alone they felt grateful.

Boudica looked at her daughter's wounds. The child had human bites all over her shoulders and her tiny rosebud nipples had been bitten right through. The blood had dried but the black and blue bruising would stay for many days to come.

Boudica had caught only a glimpse of Ceridwen's attacker, while she herself had been hauled to the feet of Suetonius by her hair. She remembered him and given only a blink of an eye's chance, she would send his soul to Andraste as a sacrifice!

Prasutagus had once told her that it would damage her spirit to hold a grudge against any man, but he was not here to see his favoured daughter treated worse than an animal. If he had been, then he too would ask the gods to accept the blood of this dreadful savage as he plunged the holy sickle into his throat.

Chapter 6

Dawn had come almost unnoticed. The grey skies with fat bellied clouds, threatened rain. The sun had remained hidden and once again Boudica was foiled. Without the sun to guide her, she could not tell in which direction they were travelling. Her nose could tell her nothing because it was still blocked with blood. She was oblivious to the scent of each tree and plant that grew, possessed its own perfume.

She tried to listen for the sounds of wild animals and birds, for each one had its own home and call, but her ears seemed to have been dulled too. The clues that she could have garnered from the very nature of her surroundings would have helped her, but she was deprived of them all, except her one usable eye.

Carefully she raised herself up high enough to see over the side of the   chariot. This time she was cautious of her right arm, using her left seemingly to ease herself into a better sitting position so as not to arouse suspicion. There was so little to see. Her left eye was almost out of its socket and the right one was blurred and could not see far. The heavy bellied flop flapping of a flock of crows caught Boudica's attention. These were the birds that heralded the bringer of death. Yes, she thought, Ceridwen and I will die and who's to tell where or how? Her heart shrivelled to think that she and her little daughter would die un-mourned in an unknown grave that is if we ever get to be buried!

The surrounding bushes along the road that the Romans had built, hid from view anything that could have been of assistance. The misty air also seemed to be against her. The gods were not going to help her. Even Andraste, the earth goddess, had not given her any assistance, only dire warnings for having ignored her advice about taking up arms against a powerful enemy.

Boudica would have felt some contentment just knowing where they were going, but all her training in the Druid Circle had been of little or no use.

Then one of the guards to whom she was anchored by a waist shackle, told her of Suetonius's plan of taking her directly to Rome by boat. His intention was to frighten her, which he did, but Boudica gave no indication that he had scored a hit. She would not give this man the satisfaction.

And then what? What plans had Suetonius plotted for her, she wondered? She knew that she would get no reprieve from him. And the traitor who had sneaked off, hiding from her wrath, where was he now? Anger stirred in her like a coiled viper. Nothing would save him if once she could lay her hands upon him, and she would haunt Julius through all eternity to make him pay for the suffering that Ceridwen had endured. For it was he who had brought Suetonius to the secret, sacred grove of ancient oaks where she and the remnants of her army had taken refuge.

Prasutagus had tried to give her advice about not letting a stranger know of its existence and she had never realised how significant that warning had been. What about Julius Classicus, the lover in the woods, had he followed her for years?

The threatening clouds overhead burst, shedding their load; as the cold, stinging drops fell upon Boudica's face, they sent nauseating pain zigzagging across her brain. They hit the damaged eye and broken arm and sent the blood flowing from the wounds again. Ceridwen tore off a strip of cloth from her shift and gently dabbed at Boudica's injuries, trying not to cause her mother further pain. The luxury of gritting her teeth was denied to Boudica because the loose ones were now starting to fall out and the remainder were throbbing painfully.

The fast march metered out by Suetonius's for his army and the rumbling of the chariot, seemed to go on for days without stopping for rest or food. There were six armed guards now who ran at the sides of the cart. Iron shackles held Boudica's good arm and the broken one was fastened to theirs, as well as the binding rope about her upper torso. Suetonius was determined that his captives would never escape his jurisdiction. He would take them to Rome and present them to his Emperor himself.

With a stifled groan Boudica eased her head back down again, being careful not to nudge the worst injuries. The aches and pains in her abused body were swamped by the soul stabbing agony in her right arm.

"Andraste, I beg of you, give me the courage not to weep," Boudica prayed, but a sob of anguish escaped her raw throat.

Suetonius would wreak his revenge for the loss of his troops that she and her followers had killed in battle, and the insult that she had thrown at him when he questioned the whereabouts of her elder daughter Cavatina. What he would do to them, made even her strong heart tremble with dread.

She knew only too well what she would do if the tables had been turned and no mistake, but not this torture of breaking her arm without cauterising the stump, which was a cold-blooded and most painful murder and an insult to a monarch. That should never have happened.

Feeling sick and weary with the old chariot bouncing and jolting on the hard packed mud and cobblestone Roman road, Boudica closed her one good eye as Ceridwen nursed her on her lap. She let her memory float back to the first time that she had seen Prasutagus...

After a smooth crossing of the Mare Germanicum that surrounded the north of the country of Britain, the longboat approached the gently sloping pebbly beach where a crowd of people waited for a glimpse of their new

27

queen. Her oldest brother Sven stood upright at her back to give comfort. His face with its thick red bushy brows and beard, the dark red thatch on his head cascading over his shoulders and tunic, and the heavy bronze helmet held in place by the strong leather strap, all gave the impression that he was a ferocious warrior, which indeed he was, yet Boudica had known nothing but kindness from him.

Even though Sven's father was a High Chieftain of the Vikings, he preferred to roam the high seas and work as an oarsman than sit idly in the great hall. He was built like a giant with a deep muscled chest and strong legs. His arms were like huge pillars developed by the rowing of the longboats over stormy seas.

Sven placed a huge, calloused hand on her shoulder and whispered a few words of encouragement to her. She smiled gaily and lifted her chin. She looked about the land ahead of her. The day was grey and overcast. Boudica had never seen such dullness. The people, the sea and land all seemed to be in a depressing fog.

Alesund, her Norseland home in the district of Vestalandet, was always windswept. The warm seas that crashed against the rocky headlands were the colour of the mid-day sky. The mountains were snow tipped even in the summer, and the lower slopes were covered with trees a deeper shade of green than grass. The fishing provided a rich living. Her brother Sven and other young men knew where the sea sent the warm currents of water and brought the cod and herring in great shoals, filling the nets with the seas bounty. They traded with the farmers who lived to the south. They were always ready to do a deal with them for fish and great pine trees to make furniture and exchange stock.

The pine trees that grew tall and straight in the forest made them the best for boat building too, Alesund was an industrious and wealthy town and now this dreary land of the Iceni was to be her new home!

Boudica glanced along at the gathering, and noticed one man who stood at the front, head and shoulders above the rest. His cloak was of a deep rich red, threaded with gold and the spear he carried was huge, so that it made him stand out from the crowd.

His face was free of any beard, yet he was not a fresh-faced young boy. His world-weary eyes betrayed the fact that he was closer to her father's age than hers. His hair had been cut to his shoulders and was light brown in colour. The harp that he carried as if it were a part of his dress was slung over his left shoulder by a leather thong.

Her father had told her of the custom of the men of this land of the Britons who shaved their faces. They had no need to guard against the bitter cold winds of the north, as he had, when they went hunting the wild white bear, boar or caribou or fishing off the rocky coasts in the wild oceans.

Back in her home, wolves were usually hunted at the fall of leaves when the coats of the young dog wolves were thick and glossy. The pine marten were trapped at the same time, but only the pelts of young males were kept to make the linings of the winter clothes, so that the females who carried young would live to give birth to the next generation and so ensure a continuous supply of pelts. Such as these were the ones that had gone to make up the cloak that Boudica wore to meet her betrothed. Boudica had not wanted to leave the home of her mother and father, but this was now forgotten.

Chapter 7

She had been so happy with her crowd of brothers, going hunting, fishing and fighting mock battles. They had taught her how to use a sword and spear to great effect, just as if she were a man. They had also shown her the weakest places to hit a man who would attempt to deflower her. "Hit them in the throat little sister; they will give up their quest soon enough then."

Those had been happy days indeed. Her father was a good-hearted man, had explained to her the ways of diplomacy and that with her marriage to such a prosperous and influential man as Prasutagus, she would ensure the peace and trade between the two countries.

King Prasutagus of the Iceni was very wealthy and still without a wife. Her father also explained that Prasutagus was many years older than she was, but he was kind and would take good care of her. It was the best match that he could arrange for her since she had lived for eighteen summers and it was well past the time for her to have a husband. She would become Queen of the Iceni.

Before Boudica left her native land to journey to that of Prasutagus, there had been an immense feast to celebrate the betrothal. Mead and ale had run like water in the great hall of the Viking lord and the rune master had been called to tell of the integrity of the marriage. He had cast the stones and foretold a happy, successful marriage, blessed by two children, and Boudica would live longer than her husband.

Abruptly, he had stopped, looked away furtively and insisted that the stones were without further knowledge. He would say no more. Her father had looked deeply troubled by the sudden cessation of information from the rune master. He said, that once his beloved Boudica had a sensible husband to care for her, any childish foolishness that she might indulge in would soon be diverted, especially when she became a mother. All women seemed to settle down once they had a baby in their arms to care for.

So it was that Boudica left the snowy mountains of her home in Alesund, and travelled south, hugging the coast line and then crossed the Mere Germanium at its narrowest point, to join Prasutagus in Anglia.

Two other long boats with their occupants of Viking warriors and serving maids were accompanied by the Bride Gifts of skins of the great white bear, gold mined from the rivers of ice in the far north, shaped into drinking mugs and platters, and teeth of ancient animals found in the permafrost frost, that had been artfully carved with hunting scenes. Boudica was a Viking Princess and the gifts to King Prasutagus of the Iceni were of the most valued in Boudica's land.

The flotilla drifted with the current alongside the jetty and gently bumped against the lead boat. Sven had no difficulty keeping his balance, but Boudica needed to hold her brother's arm for support.

She had never liked the tossing waves. Her stomach refused to accept the restless motion, and she would feel sick even on the shortest of sea journeys. The group escorting her had gone along the shore as far south as the land of Germanica north of Gaul, before they had taken her across the sea in the sturdy long boat, because it was the shortest journey over the ever-restless seas.

The wood and stone jetty ran several arms lengths out into the sea and it would facilitate an easy landing for the travellers. Her brother Sven held her hand to steady her first step on foreign soil. It would be a very bad omen if anything marred her first footfall in her new home of Icenorum Venta.

The tall man passed his spear to a dark skinned guard who Boudica was later to learn was a slave by the name of Shar. Prasutagus had bought Shar to save him from having his hamstrings severed because he had run away from a malicious master. Shar was Prasutagus' protector and was almost as tall as his new master.

As Prasutagus strode forward, he held out his extraordinarily long arms, and with one of his huge hands took one of Boudica's in his, whilst he placed the other under her elbow. This made it perfectly clear to all who were watching, that this woman belonged to him, their king… Prasutagus; he had come to lay claim to his bride.

With a slight toss of her head, she threw off the hood of her magnificent wolf skin cloak that hung from her shoulders to the tips of her toes. Once free of the restrictions of the cowl, the beauty of her apple blossom skin, small even teeth and long curling, amber hair with its circlet of gold were exposed.

The wind ruffled a stray lock playfully, to dance in the breeze, and just then a weak sun came from behind the clouds. The grey mist glowed with the muted rainbow colours of nacre that reflected the loveliness of the young princess. The watching crowd gasped with delight at the sight of a girl so young and comely who had come to be their queen. She was like a visitation of a goddess.

Her tunic was of the palest cream coloured wool that had been embroidered by willing and crafty hands. It was held at her waist by a girdle of woven black and red wool, in the symbols of the runes that prophesied a loving marriage, blessed by two children.

Her dark grey eyes rested momentarily on the soft, pale blue ones of Prasutagus, to fathom out his thoughts of her. Would he accept her as his queen, or was this a convenient marriage for him to beget his heirs?

He was only half a head taller than she was, and at that moment as they exchanged glances, Boudica became his slave. Never would she be free of the spell that bound her to Prasutagus. She was his until death parted them. Prasutagus had exercised his most potent gift, that of a hypnotist. He was also the most talented seer and healer in all the land of the Celtic nation that stretched from the southern most tip of Gaul to the far north of Boudica's home land.

Then a beam of a smile played about her lips as a look of pure rapture lifted the dullness from the sombre eyes of Prasutagus and a joyous grin lit up his face.

So, my king is a man of deep feelings and can be moved by a woman's beauty, she thought. Then she lowered her eyes so as not to betray her secret thoughts to him.

Chapter 8

Boudica smiled and murmured as she lay in a deep coma...Prasutagus! He had been so wrong in believing that she could not love him without the chains of hypnosis. Even when he had disclosed the real reason for marrying her was that he needed to strengthen his blood line by marrying outside the Icine tribe for a truly healthy heir; her love had not turned to hate, for she had found that he was a true and honest man to be respected.

The jostling of the chariot impinged on her dreams, taking her back to the time when she and Prasutagus had travelled to the Great Circle of Stones for the midsummer solstice ceremony. They were also to declare their vows of marriage before the Druids' High Priests and the whole company of those Celtics gathered there.

Prasutagus picked some of his best hunter-warriors and two ladies to wait on Boudica. The men were to set up camps, act as guards and supply fresh meat whenever it was needed.

Her brother Sven was to be witness to the marriage and place her hand in that of Prasutagus, thus formally announcing that the Viking princess Boudica was now the bride of Prasutagus, King of the Iceni.

The journey took the cortège several days as they travelled west and southwards towards the setting sun.

In an attempt to ease her concern about her future life in Britain, Prasutagus told her something of his early life with the Druids and the rules that governed them, how he had not seen his home or family for twenty winters. This was why he had not married sooner.

It was a long and difficult training, but as time had gone by he had grown to appreciate the doctrine and the remarkable lessons that he and the other pupils had learned, none of which was ever written on parchment or told to any outside the Druid Circle.

Prasutagus told Boudica of one fair skinned, blue eyed youth there who joined them when he was barely twelve years of age. "He came from the land near Egypt, though his birthplace was a mystery to him. His parents emigrated to Egypt while he was still in swaddling clothes. Then when he was old enough to leave home, he was brought to Britain by his uncle Joseph, who was a merchant interested in obtaining tin from the mines in the western regions. The uncle paid well for his tuition and instructed the Guardian Druid to take care of the youth for he was a source of great love. He proved to be the best acolyte that the mentors ever taught. The young man had profound abilities to heal the sick. His hands had only to touch a lame man and he would be walking again. A woman brought her baby son to him to cure the child of a coughing fever, but when our tutor examined it, he was pronounced dead!

"This was sad news indeed. The mother could not accept the statement and insisted that he held her baby in his arms. He took the lifeless child and smiled. Such compassion I have never seen before or since," said Prasutagus. As this young man's eyes alighted on the mother, he said, 'Your love and faith have given you back your child. Go in love and worship the one who gives life to all. Your child will live and be a blessing to all who meet him,' then he gave the live baby back to its mother. She bowed her head as if he were a king, and attempted to thank him. But he stopped her and told her that he was a path. It was her love for her child that was the power of healing!

"So wonderful were this man's talents that when he returned to his parents' home at the age of thirty two, many of those in high office felt threatened by him and schemed his downfall, saying that he was a heretic and also plotted to overthrow the Roman government. Inevitably he was soon betrayed by a friend and was crucified at the orders of Claudius."

Prasutagus paused as he thought deeply at the fate of such an intelligent and enlightened person, and decided that if a friend could delude and betray *him*, then anyone could be deceived!

The weather was kind and mild, the early spring sun had begun to contain some warmth as the cavalcade made its way ever south, stopping at the homes of other kings or local overlords for the evening, where Prasutagus and his betrothed were made welcome with great feasts. Boudica was excited to know her husband to be was such a powerful and respected man throughout the lands of Britain.

Gifts were exchanged and Boudica found herself laden with jewels and fine cloth. However, she began to feel the overpowering desire to lie down and sleep the moon and sun round, instead of climbing up into the chariot that Prasutagus handled with familiar dexterity.

The hunting parties that set forth to gather meat from the forests to provision the feasts, were a merry affair. No more animals were slaughtered than were needed to feed the towns-people where they were staying, and a roasting fire of hot embers was always waiting for the return of the huntsmen. If she had not felt as if she were travelling to the ends of the earth, Boudica would have been blissfully happy.

Eventually, when they had finally arrived at the Great Circle, Boudica was shown the cowhide tent where she could rest and refresh herself after such a long journey. She removed the cloak that had been her bed covering as well as protection from the chill winds that blew in from the plains as well as the high hills, then rinsed her hands and face in the soft well water using the herb scented soap that the Celts were renowned for, and the Romans found valuable in their baths.

Britain, Boudica decided, was a cold and damp land. She thought longingly of the warm winds that came from the sea off Vestalandet, where Haugesund was situated, with the deep and steep walled, narrow rocky fiords, where the water was warm enough to swim in nearly all year long. She yearned to feel the caress of the refreshing water to take the ache from her limbs.

After a brief rest, her waiting ladies and she wandered around the outside of the Great Circle. She realised that the gathering was the largest the she had ever seen. A fair trade in food and sweetmeats was going on while harpers sang songs of the coming marriage of Prasutagus and her. Word of her beauty had reached them by way of pot menders and travelling bands of farm workers. Boudica laughed with merriment at their efforts and the harpers in turn smiled their thanks of her approval of their strivings and inventiveness.

She noticed that Druid priests from all the Celtic lands were there, from the southern most point of Gaul to her homeland. Later when Prasutagus joined her and her waiting ladies, they were greeted many times. Boudica also noticed the secret sign of fingers held at the wrist, used to greet a fellow Druid. It was passed between the elders of the hierarchy of Bards and Prasutagus. She was curious but not unduly concerned, Prasutagus was a man of many great talents. This much had been revealed to her as they had mingled among the other tribes. The honest good wishes had been of respect, as if he were a grand master of the Druids.

Chapter 9

The music and dancing by the younger people gathered outside the wooden circle, which encompassed the Great Stone Circle, was gay, and Boudica's feet were itching to be away and join them. Her tiredness was forgotten but she knew she must restrain her exuberance as her place was at Prasutagus's side with her maids. Sven and the guards were close by. She must stay with Prasutagus and be introduced to all the Druid high priests.

Their wedding ceremony was to be held as soon as the first rays of the summer sun had cleared the first great stone arch the following morning.

Prasutagus had been careful of all the unwritten laws and had respected her chastity. He would not claim her as his wife until after they had each given and accepted the vows of love and loyalty to each other.

As the long evening drew to a close and the night shadows lengthened Boudica and her handmaidens left the men to their discussions and went to the leather tent to sleep. This was the last time they would undo her girdle and remove her shift and long linen breeches imposed by her mother.

Boudica welcomed the sight of her tent. She was near to complete exhaustion, and all that she could think of was to close her eyes until morning.

A candle of pure bees wax had been lit and placed on a small table. Her mirror of beaten and polished bronze, a hog's hair brush and comb that had been carved from the tusk of a gigantic whale was also there. The teeth of the comb had been so finely cut that her hair needed to be combed most carefully so as not to pull on a tangle. A thick sheep's skin fleece lay on the grassy earth, and her wolf skin cloak lay where she could cover herself if she needed it against the night-chilled air.

The maids came in with her to comb the long gold and bronze hair that hung to her waist. Water had been warmed and a tablet of scented soap provided for her to wash the grime of the day from her face, hands and feet.

They glanced knowingly at each other, smiling while they assisted her to undress and asked her if her mother had given her instruction as what to expect from a husband. Boudica laughed with them and said, "Yes, my mother is not the fool to let me make a marriage bed without my knowing that a man is no different from a stallion!" She tossed her hair from her shoulders and gave them an enigmatic look to assure them that she was indeed quite knowledgeable.

The fatigue that she had felt earlier because of all the events of the past few weeks, slipped away. Boudica was too tense to sleep. Her mind kept returning to Prasutagus. Where was he? What was he doing? What did he really think of her? Would he still look at her tomorrow morning as if he adored her?

Suddenly she was awake, not realising that she had actually slept. The night was starting to give way to the dawn. Her maids were gently shaking her by her shoulder. It was time for her to be dressed in her very best shift of pure white cotton with its gold thread. The wolf skin cloak was placed about her shoulders against the early morning chill.

The morning air was grey and cool. People stood silently in their appointed places inside the wooden circle, and only the high priests waited inside the Great Stone Circle, Prasutagus among them.

He was wearing a magnificent gold helmet that was carved and chaste with mythical creatures. Never had she seen so much grandeur, and Prasutagus seemed to stand even taller that usual.

In the early morning gloom he beckoned to her to join him, and slowly she came to his side. Fear of what was expected of her as well as the stillness of the huge crowd, made her shiver.

Prasutagus placed a sympathetic arm across her shoulders and glanced down to smile at her. She looked at him squarely and wondered if he understood the knot of fear that gripped her stomach. Did he realise that she was doing her father's bidding, and that she was only marrying the Iceni king to seal a bond of friendship, promoting peace between the Vikings and the British? The feelings that she had for him were unusual to her. Could this be love, she wondered?

The Druid priests, Prasutagus and Boudica stood in line, waiting for the sun god to rise over the distant hills. A harper began to pluck the strings of the instrument that he carried slung over his shoulder the same way as Prasutagus carried his.

The music from the strings came sensitively at first, and then grew in timbre and volume as other harpers took up the theme. A young man sang words of praise to the sun as it sent an aura of red and yellow across the dawn sky. The very stones of the Stone Circle seemed to take up the theme, sending the harmony out into those waiting in the Wooden Circle, then out across the meadows.

Boudica could feel the old sentinel stones quake with the music, and as they too took up the song. The air around trembled. The music grew louder until the sound echoed off the hills and valleys.

What magic is this, Boudica wondered? Such strange things happened in this land of the Britons.

First the sky gradually turned a rosy pink, the last of the night clouds catching the rays of the summer sun. Then the sun climbed into the sky in all his majesty, and warmth crept with the encroaching rays.

As she watched the magnificence of the mighty sun god mount the heavens, covering all with his benevolence, excitement bubbled inside Boudica like a rippling spring of water to replace the anxiety she had felt at the dawn.

40

The music swelled then suddenly ceased and a hush fell over the circle and surrounding fields.

Prasutagus removed his helmet and bowed his head, covering his eyes as he did so to protect them against the mighty fires of the sun god. It was well known that whoever looked upon the glorious face of the sun would lose their sight forever. The gold of his helmet would surely attract his anger and cook his brains to stew.

Prasutagus knelt and placed his spear upon the green sward. It seemed to Boudica as though the spear was his staff of office. He kept his head low, indicating to Boudica to do the same.

Gradually as the sun ascended and stood above the first arch stones, Prasutagus turned to her and lifted her to her feet again. His eyes glowed with an inner fire, and his face was serious. "We can be married now, my beloved Boudica, or not. The choice is yours, you are free to decide." Once again, Prasutagus was obeying the Druid laws of venerating the feminine sex as the representative of the earth goddess. Never would he take her to his bed against her wishes.

Her blood was like burning pitch in her veins. She was of eighteen summers and no man had entered her. Her mother forbade her ever to encourage a young man to remove her dress, or allow a man to remove the long breeches made of linen that she wore night and day. Her maidenhood was of more value than her obvious beauty, and if she disobeyed, then her father would sell her to the first trader who called.

Mother told the truth. As much as father loved her, his royal house and he would be disgraced if she allowed herself to be deflowered by a common felon, as had her older sister who had disappeared along with the travelling merchants when they had visited two years previously.

Boudica breathed deeply and nodded her assent. The crown of her golden hair with its restraining circlet, caught

41

and reflected and sun's rays. Not being able to voice the confusion that she felt, there were no words for what she experienced at that moment, and tears glistened on her eyelashes.

Chapter 10

Prasutagus motioned for Sven to join them as he led Boudica towards the waiting High Priest, Leofric. Sven took her hands from those of Prasutagus and Leofric asked her if she was a willing bride. This time she answered loud and clear so that all assembled could hear her proclamation. Not a sound could be heard from the great throng that had gathered about the Great Circle for the first day of the summer solstice and the marriage of the Iceni king, as they waited expectantly for Boudica's reply.

"Yes, I take Prasutagus for my husband for all our lives together," Boudica declared.

"I take Boudica for my wife for evermore," was his inscrutable reply. His fathomless eyes held those of Boudica and seemed to hold a mystery that he would never tell. Then Sven passed Boudica's hands back to Prasutagus.

Prasutagus beckoned to the dark skinned Shar, his man at arms who had stood waiting for the signal to bring his master a small, soft leather bag. Prasutagus put his hand inside and brought out a heavy torque of twisted gold. He asked Boudica to lift her hair from her shoulders and placed the golden gift around her neck. "This is my symbol of love," he said, and it would tell all who saw it that Boudica was Queen of the Iceni, wife of Prasutagus. Then took her fingertips to his mouth and kissed them, his eyes never leaving her face and his glance held a message of deep desire.

Boudica lowered her gaze. She turned to her brother and Sven placed a gold brooch-pin with silver runes of love knots and good health embedded in the gold, into her outstretched hand. It also contained a strange jewel that changed colours as the sun's rays caught it. The greenish blue gem came from beyond the high mountains to the

43

east of her birth country and was greatly valued as a bringer of good luck and long life. Boudica fixed the pin to Prasutagus's deep red and gold threaded cloak, high on the shoulder where it could be seen, for this too was a symbol of love.

Whilst Prasutagus held onto the hand of his new bride, High Priest Leofric placed a wreath of ivy and mistletoe about the head of Prasutagus and thornless rose blossoms and honeysuckle on Boudica's. The ivy and mistletoe denoted Prasutagus's virility and everlasting love for his bride. The rose and honeysuckle stood for Boudica's beauty and her necessity to hold onto her husband for support.

Then Leofric chanted something in a tongue that Boudica did not understand, with sibilant flute like tones accompanying words that seemed to float on the morning breeze towards the whole assembly. She wondered if it was the forbidden language of the lost people who, she had been told, had made the Great Stone Circle.

Leofric held up Boudica's free hand and announced to the gathering that now she was the wife of Prasutagus, she was also to be admitted into the Druid Circle of Enlightenment where she would be allowed to study those gifts of the gods that showed most promise in her.

A full-grown ram was lead forward, a wreath of poppies about his curled horns. The animal was in its prime, full of life and vigour. The high priest motioned for it to be laid on the flat altar stone. The ram hardly struggled against its captors, but put its head low on the stone as if in submission to its fate.

Leofric drew a silver and bronze curved knife from his robe. His aim was pure and true. The throat of the sacrificial ram was slit without needing a second attempt. The animal died swiftly and cleanly, its blood caught in a gold chalice. This Leofric offered first to the sun god, then with ceremony poured it onto the grassy ground as an offering to Andraste, the earth goddess. The rich, healthy ram's blood would be an acceptable tribute to her, giving the promise that the marriage was certain to be blessed with children. Prasutagus kissed his new bride on the brow and turned to present her to the gathering.

The priest clapped his hands and the magic spell of silence was broken. The applause was spontaneous and the cheers were loud and jovial. Well-wishers came forward and jostled Boudica and Prasutagus, laughing and joking as wedding guests always had and always would. A harper sang a ballad to the beauty of Boudica and the majesty of Prasutagus, and foretold a happy union.

The dancing, singing and feasting lasted until the sun had attained its noon, when Prasutagus informed Leofric that he would soon be ready to take Boudica back to his kingdom.

Prasutagus gave the orders to Sven that the handmaidens and one of the guards were to take some of the packhorses and chariots that were now heavily laden with wedding gifts and return to Icenorum Venta in East Anglia.

Some panniers were placed over the saddle of one horse and loaded with provisions; Boudica's wolf skin cloak was placed in the racing chariot that Prasutagus favoured, in readiness for her to use if the journey proved cold. Prasutagus also took a pair of unburdened geldings for himself and his new bride to ride when they wished to be alone, and with Shar in attendance behind Prasutagus, they rode in procession until they were well out of sight of the henge.

Sven was now ready to leave his young sister in the care of her new husband. The kindly king had treated Sven and his entourage with respect as was due to a visiting prince and he had noted the deference with which Prasutagus had treated Boudica. Sven decided that Prasutagus was an honourable man to be trusted with his sister to whom he was devoted.

He prepared and marshalled the cavalcade into an orderly column to make the journey back to Icenorum Venta with as little difficulty as possible.

Chapter 11

Sven kissed Boudica goodbye, holding on to her just long enough for her to know that he loved her dearly and would miss the little girl whom he had watched grow into a beautiful woman. They had always been good friends and he had taught her as much as he could about the use of a sword and spear and had delighted in her prowess. He wished with all his heart that Boudica would never need to use the knowledge that he had given her, yet he felt that loveliness such as hers would always attract trouble.

As Sven's group headed north by east for Iceni lands, Prasutagus took the bridle of Boudica's horse, and with Shar, the remaining guard led the way further to the west and slightly north, to a trail that was hardly discernible among the tall grasses and sapling trees.

Until now there had been very little conversation between them. Prasutagus had appeared to be deep in thought and Boudica did not feel inclined to break into his reverie. Now, however, Prasutagus gave Boudica careful appraisal with his gentle eyes. "Are you wearied, my wife?" he asked.

Boudica gave him an equally long and careful look. "Yes, my lord. It seems that we have travelled to the furthest reaches of Britain. My eyes are closing of their own accord. I trust that we will halt for the night soon?" she replied. "But tell me, why was a ram sacrificed and not a man? For such an important occasion as the midsummer solstice and our marriage vows proclaimed, I thought that nothing less would do?"

Prasutagus smiled at Boudica's blood lust. "Yes, true, but we only sacrifice felons or prisoners who we think that Andraste will accept with pleasure. The only prisoner that we have at this time is a man who has poisoned a neighbour in the hope of gaining his property. He is terrified of the retribution waiting for him in the next world. Such a person would bring bad luck to our marriage. His body will have to be burnt along with his victims so that it does not pollute the earth and offend Andraste, for she would take vengeance on such an obnoxious offering. No! The ram is a noble creature whose blood was pure. We are much blessed by his life." Prasutagus chuckled, and his face lit up with merriment. What kind of a maiden have I married, he wondered.

Eventually, Prasutagus stopped his horse and dismounted before helping Boudica to do the same. He tethered the animals to some low growing trees where they could graze on the lush summer grass. Then he gave instructions to Shar to go and catch the wild boar that had left its markings close by.

The hot midsummer sun had dried the early morning dew as Boudica walked among the tall grasses that grew so abundantly in the meadow. The heady scents of blossoms growing in the nearby hedgerow were overwhelming, making her head swim with their intoxicating perfumes.

She stooped to pick some flowers, clover, poppies and daisies, which grew in profusion. She smiled as she raised them to her face to inhale their exciting fragrance. Never had she seen such a wealth of colours.

Boudica glanced up as a shadow fell beside her to see the long, dark silhouette of Prasutagus. He moved towards her languidly. His eyes half closed, never left her as he watched her inhale the scents of summer. He held out his hand and led her gently to where a brook purled among some low growing bushes of flowering hawthorn.

"Come, sit a while and take some fruit and mead," he said, offering her a cup of honeyed wine. Boudica sank to her knees gratefully and cradled the flowers on her lap. They were so beautiful, she thought as she glanced down at them.

Boudica was feeling so weary and exhausted. She felt as if she could sleep till the moon was renewed. She leaned her back against the trunk of a slender birch tree. Her throat was dry as tinder and the mead tasted so sweet that she drank it down and held the cup out for more.

"Not yet my love. Have some fruit first," said Prasutagus as he offered her some yellow fruit that she did not recognise. Like the mead, it was exceptionally sweet. The juice ran down Boudica's chin. She chuckled and rolled over onto her back on the mossy ground, then gazed up at the fading sunset.

"See, the sun god is on his way to the land of sleep. Where will we sleep tonight, my lord?" she asked, her eyes gazing lovingly into his.

"I will show you, Boudica, but I will have to extract a promise from you first, for this is a secret held only by the kings of the Iceni for hundreds of years and must never be shared," he said. He would have continued, but he was interrupted by Shar, returning with the carcass of the boar. It was a plump, young male. Prasutagus did not get the opportunity to finish his instructions to Boudica. Shar slapped the animal's flank. He was laughing, and his dark brown eyes twinkled with merriment. "The flesh will be sweet and tender when it has been roasted over hot embers," he commented.

This was the first time that Boudica had heard him speak except to acknowledge his lord and master's commands. She was pleasantly surprised by the soft whisper that told of his birth in a far distant land.

After the skin had been scored and laced with bog mint, the carcass was roasted over a blazing fire. The pork was indeed tender. The wild herbs had enhanced the flavour better than Boudica thought possible with something so simple. She would have to remember this for when she entertained guests in Prasutagus's villa as his wife.

The three sat around the fire in companionship. Shar offered Prasutagus the sweetbreads, which he accepted on a short knife that he kept on his belt, and placed the tasty morsel on the gold platter by his side. Then he asked Boudica if there was any special part of the flesh that she preferred?

"Yes, I would like the short ribs at the middle." These had always seemed to her the most delicate cut of meat in any animal.

After he had given his mistress a large slice of her chosen cut, Shar asked Prasutagus if he might have a leg with the feet. To Shar's way of thinking, it was the only part worth the effort of roasting, the feet with the gelatinous gristle, something to get his teeth into and the plump haunch, so tasty! He would not waste the juices on a platter, even that of gold and proceeded to sink his small, sharp teeth into the rump of the boar,

The hot fat ran down their chins and smeared their faces. They ate their fill and laughing at the enjoyment of the food and goblets of mead, until only the head and bones remained.

As evening drew on, they had eaten as much as their stomachs would hold. Prasutagus said, "Shar, bury the fragments, and make certain that the fire is dead. We do not need anyone to know that we have been here. Also I believe that Andraste will welcome the rest of our feast," and he proceeded to help Shar carry some water from the stream to extinguish the smouldering embers. They covered the scar with earth, which Shar had turned over when he had buried the debris of their banquet.

Chapter 12

Mounting her horse again was a tremendous effort for Boudica as she was so tired. Her stomach was full and the mead had gone straight to her head. The sun had all but vanished from the darkening sky.

Prasutagus led her horse gently to where the forest had grown thick in a deep gully. There was only one way in and Shar would stand guard there. Helping Boudica to alight, he held her in his arms, his face close to hers. There was a fleeting look of craving that she had seen in the eyes of so many young men when they looked her way and she knew that he would soon appease this longing. All Boudica wanted to do was to lie down and sleep.

Prasutagus knew that he would have to be wary of the fact that Boudica was a virgin. His knowledge of such matters had been learned at the halls of the Druids. It was deemed necessary for all men to understand the workings of a woman's mind and body to prepare them for the outside world as loving and considerate husbands and fathers. Therefore he took her kindly by the hand and led her to where a dense forest of oak trees grew in a valley protected on three sides by high rocky cliffs. It was very thick, old woodland that had been ancient before the arrival of the Roman hordes.

The trees grew so densely that there was no room for the light of the setting sun to reach through and shed its soft glow. The path that they travelled had been made by animals over the centuries and was scarcely to be seen in the gloom.

Boudica watched carefully where her husband placed his feet, always one foot directly in front of the other. His cloak had been tucked up into his waistband so that it did not even brush against the low growing ferns and grasses. She followed suit and upon looking back the way that they had come, could see no trace of their passing.

He walked in silence as he led his bride along the twisting narrow path through the wild foliage, to the centre of a glade where the trees were so deformed in their growth, they looked as if they had been there since the world began.

The branches traced a leafy canopy overhead and the fallen leaves of many winters littered the floor, making it a place of complete stillness. Even the animals had hushed their sounds.

The trunks of these guardian-protecting trees were covered with lichens. Their roots ploughed deep into the bosom of the earth, forming a ridge of high banks that surrounded the centre of the dell like a comforting womb of the earth goddess.

Prasutagus had retrieved the wolf skin cloak and carried it over his arm to the open space in the forest, and now he laid his long red cloak on the mossy bank by one of the tree trunks. Then he took Boudica's hand and sat her down.

Taking the harp that he carried slung over his shoulder, Prasutagus smiled at his bride and began to sing her a lullaby, the words of which at first eluded her, but somewhere in the dim recesses of her mind, Boudica knew that she had heard this melody before. It was plaintive, as if a lover was calling to his beloved to come home.

Then he came closer. His pale blue eyes filled her vision, and his full lips formed the words plainly:

The touch of a blossom petal, this is my love,

The sigh of a summer breeze, this is my love,

The bells of blue in the spring, this is my love,

The smile of a happy child, this is my love,

Come my beloved, come to my heart,

Come and accept this treasure that I bring to you…

His voice dropped to a whisper as the last of the resonance faded and without taking his eyes from her, Prasutagus offered her a golden goblet of mead that tasted of mint and fruit. She detected a slightly bitter aftertaste that the honey could not quite disguise. Boudica tried to think what it could be, but her mind no longer belonged to her. It was wafting high in the trees, looking in the birds' nests that were wedged so precariously between the twigs on the top most branches.

She peered down at her resting body lying on Prasutagus's cloak. He had unrolled her wolf-skin cape to cover them, and then lay down beside her. Gently, he stroked her soft maiden's cheek, and kissed her lips tenderly.

"Boudica," he whispered, "this is a very sacred place, and I bring you here to prove that I trust you well enough. Promise me that you will never divulge to anyone its whereabouts."

Boudica attempted to murmur her understanding of what he was saying but her spirit soared above the clouds.

"This is our secret," he was telling her. "This is where our children will be conceived. This is where you will always be able to come in times of trouble. Trust no one else with this place, for it could one day save your life." Prasutagus had looked earnestly into her eyes as if to imprint his plea into her memory.

Boudica's gaze was vacant and as hard as she tried, she could not bring herself to understand why it was so important. She knew that he was deeply concerned. Did he really see the future, she wondered, and then started to laugh nervously, as her mind dwelt on the prospect of such an old man entering her. Yet when she looked at Prasutagus in the moonlight that filtered through the summer-young oak leaves, he appeared to have become a young and handsome man in his prime!

At first their lovemaking was slow and affectionate. Prasutagus took great care not to tear her maidenhead too painfully, and although the wine had blurred her awareness, Boudica knew that Prasutagus was being as kind and loving as any man possibly is on such an occasion.

The surprise came without warning when the irresistible desire of Boudica's young body overcame her ignorance, and she responded to Prasutagus's lovemaking so vehemently, that even he was startled. She had embraced him with arms and legs wrapped forcefully around his torso so that she felt as if she would crush him to death.

A scream, unbidden, escaped from her. Boudica was no longer in control of her mind or body, and she writhed on Prasutagus's cape, demented.

Prasutagus had buried his seed deep in her loins. It was accepted by her waiting womb greedily, and she knew as most women before her knew, that at that moment a child was conceived.

When the violent shudder that had engulfed her subsided, she released him to breath in deep gulps of life-giving air. The wolf skin cloak lay unwanted as perspiration drenched them both.

Prasutagus looked at her as if he had never even suspected that his bride could harbour such passion. "My love," he said, "when I watched you alight from the longboat as my betrothed, pale skinned and ethereal looking, a visitor from the gods, I never dreamt that you would be so passionate and different from the women of my own land!"

As she snuggled down to sleep, she glanced up to see that his eyes were now wary and uncertain, as he looked at Boudica in the dim light of the stars, with consternation.

Chapter 13

Boudica smiled in her sleep, and sighed as she thought of all her mother had told her about becoming a wife. Yes, Prasutagus was much like a stallion, as her mother had predicted, but what mystery was this that made her, a virgin act so ardently? Was this Andraste's way of making childbirth more probable? Could no woman resist her husband's love?

As a shaft of moonlight pierced the canopy of young oak leaves, Boudica awoke with a raging thirst. Her mouth was acrid dry and her throat felt so sore she thought perhaps she was sickening for a fever.

Prasutagus was already awake. Seeing her discomfort, he seemed to know what ailed her. He helped her to her feet and led her by the hand through the darkness along a path only he could see. A sound of water splashing came to Boudica's ears. It grew louder as they approached a glade that opened up to the sky and the light of the new moon lit up a scene that captivated Boudica. A waterfall gushed from the top of a rocky precipice to splash down into a large pool, then meandered through a chasm and formed smaller rocky pools as it progressed.

The silver and blue of the young moon filtered down through the trees and ferns that grew so abundantly where there was a constant supply of moisture. They had been nurtured by the life-giving humidity and towered above all the others in the forest. Ferns grew in profusion, with deep cushions of moss growing between the rock-strewn loam.

The imprints of animals and birds that came to drink their fill could only just be seen in the dim light, and Boudica felt the enchantment of this blessed grove, where she too would quench her thirst.

Most of the larger boulders strewn around the clearing were smooth and rounded. Aeons of washing by tumbling water had eroded them. The smaller ones were not much bigger than pebbles, except for one large flat-topped rock that stood just in front of Boudica, away from the running water. It looked similar to the flat stone at the Great Circle and seemed to her to guard the entrance to the grotto.

The reverberation of splashing water echoed around the high cliff making speech impossible, and Boudica could only smile her delight and thanks to Prasutagus. He was still holding her hand to guide her safely through the turbulent stream to where it would be safe for her to drink and quench her thirst.

However Boudica had other ideas. She released her hand and walked boldly through the rushing waters to where a rounded boulder stood clear of the heaviest falling water, but still sent a spray out to drench it. She climbed up on to the boulder and sat where she could drink and wash away the sweat from the lovemaking. Then standing upright, she raised her hands above her head to enjoy the luxury of the cold water caressing her young body.

She glanced back to where Prasutagus should be standing, but he was well within the dark shadows and there was no sign of him. Boudica sensed that his pale blue eyes were watching her. Sitting down again, she grabbed handfuls of wet hair and proceeded to wring it as if she were at the wash trough wringing out linen.

Prasutagus inched away from his cover among the thickly growing ferns. He held his cloak out to her to protect her from the coolness of the early dawn. She came towards him smiling, trembling, but not because of the chill of cold water. She held out her hand to him.

The moonlight reflected from the pearly drops of water still clinging to her and she felt enchanted by the scene in the pallid moonlight. The kindly luminosity of the young moon made Prasutagus look so much more youthful in the night shadows and Boudica went to his arms gladly. He sat her down upon the flat stone and stood before her.

Then he embraced her and the warmth of his body melted her tremors as he held her close.

There was no honeyed wine and no fallen soft leaves but their lovemaking was even more possessed than before, and when they came to awareness again Prasutagus, his face dewed with perspiration, needed to prop himself up from the stone for support as he disentangled himself from Boudica's stifling embrace, to take in deep breaths of air.

He seemed to enjoy his roll of husband and Boudica smiled her love for him. She was learning quickly about what really pleased a man, and her lord was a man, the same as any other!

"My lady takes pleasure in a cold bath, but she should consider the possibility of our love bearing fruit," he admonished her. "We can come here when next we visit the Stone Circle which will be when the Sun starts to make the nights longer," he said, as she stood up for him to dab the last of the moisture from her roseate plump limbs with his cloak.

"And my lord should have noticed that I did not swim as a fish in the lake. Rather, I did as you say, consider the fruit of my womb!" Her unfathomable smile caused a bewildered look to cross Prasutagus's face.

"Do you know something more than I, wife?" he asked in consternation.

"Only that as a stallion mounts a mare to produce a colt, you my lord performed your duty with great pleasure it seemed, and it is with such joy that a child can be conceived," Boudica answered with mock severity, a scheming smile playing about her face. Prasutagus laughed heartily at her indirect compliment to his virility.

He must be content with that reply, she decided mentally. I will tell him that he has an heir when I think that he needs some good news.

Prasutagus sat down on the boulder again and held his hand out to her. As she grasped it, he sat her on his lap

"The gods have been kind to give you to me as a wife, Boudica. Your Viking blood runs hot and I am no longer a youth," he whispered in her ear, and then brushed a strand of damp hair from her bare shoulder to kiss it. "I think that we are given tasks by the gods to do and it is when they are completed that we are allowed to leave this life to journey on."

Prasutagus pursed his full lips and continued, "I cannot but wonder what role you will play in this life Boudica. His intelligent eyes gazed into hers as if he were trying to fathom her thoughts and knowledge. "So what did the gods intend for you when they directed you to come to me and the Iceni?"

"To make the great king of the Iceni happy and bear him his children, my lord," she replied with diffidence.

Boudica could not tell him everything that had been foretold at her birth by the Rune master. The god of fire and war, a star of brilliant red, had been at his zenith, giving her father reason to name her Victory, saying that if there were to be wars then she would lead a victorious army. This was something that Boudica could not tell her kind and loving husband. It would only give him grounds for concern and there was no hint of war in Britain.

Prasutagus breathed in deeply, content with her answer and held her close before releasing her, and leading her back to where they had spent the night.

The clamour made by the birds as they praised the sun for waking them, was deafening.

Chapter 14

"My lord, what do you call the wonderful wood?" Boudica asked as they stepped with caution so as to leave no trail from the forest.

"It has a very odd name, but a well deserved one: It's called Seven Snakes because of the number of vipers it holds." He glanced back at her as she placed her feet in the exact position as he had trod. "That is yet another reason to tread carefully, but you are safe enough with me, wife, for I know where they like to rest and hide, for strangely enough, they are shy creatures." He stopped and held a long tray briar aside from tearing her shift, then gently placed it back to where it had been seeking new ground.

Later as the sun mounted the heavens, gradually turning the grey of night to a glowing dawn, a fine mist formed that heralded the coming of a warm day. Prasutagus held up the red cloak with its gold thread, which bore witness to Boudica's virginity with the bloodstains. He would wear it with pride to show the proof to the High Druids to confirm that his choice of wife had been right. Boudica and Prasutagus, walked back carefully to where Shar waited for them with a fire that was roasting young trout for breakfast.

The journey back to Icenorum Venta, Prasutagus's home on the edge of Mare Germanicum, was interspersed with frequent stops for rest and more passionate, seductive lovemaking.

Boudica had found delight in the arms of her husband, much more than she had thought possible, and Prasutagus ceased to be cautious of her youth. The possibility of producing an heir became even more likely. There had also grown a wonderful rapport between them and often he stroked the comely round curves of her young body, and the long rippling hair, taking it to his lips and kissing it. "My beloved!" he said one day as they rested from an embrace, "your hair has more pull than a team of oxen!" His eyes were drowsy yet watchful. Boudica knew that he needed an heir to carry on the leadership of the Iceni and realised that once she had done this, he might lose interest in her. It was possible he doubted her suitability as a mother. That is something that my lord will find out soon enough, she mused.

On the second week of their long, roundabout passage home, Boudica could see that her husband was beginning to find the extended journey tedious. His cheerful face was now grey and showing sings of weariness, with drooping eyelids.

It was the time to tell him that he was to become a father. She told him that the fall of blood from her womb had ceased and she was, without doubt, having his child.

Boudica watched as the delight showed on Prasutagus's face. He was overjoyed, his eyes alight with happiness. The responsibility of caring for the infant, who was to be born when the sun god began to stay longer in the heavens, was a joy for them to contemplate.

Prasutagus's face displayed his astonishment! For him there was no uncertainty that he was the true father. He had broken her maiden's gate himself, and she had slept with no one else except him since the day at the Great Stone Circle.

Andraste had accepted the young ram as an offering, and when they arrived home there would be a celebration and an offering suitable for such a wonderful blessing. But first they must reach Icenorum Venta.

People of the Iceni tribe greeted the news of the forthcoming birth with great rejoicing. Their king was giving them an heir for the kingdom. There would be no arguments as to who should reign when he died. A female child would be as welcome as a male for either could inherit the throne. Boudica's part in the creation of a new baby was welcomed by the whole nation honouring her as the representative of Andraste, the earth goddess who was the goddess of all life and love.

Andraste was venerated as the giver of crops and of new life, a lamb or a child. It was Andraste, the Celtic nation believed, who made these gifts of life possible.

Prasutagus showed his appreciation by presenting her with a matched pair of gold earrings to go with the torque that he had given her at the marriage ceremony. However he forbade her to ride a chariot or take part in any games that he considered too rough for a pregnant woman. This irked Boudica. She felt stifled. I'll know not to tell my lord too soon if there is another child to be born, she reflected!

As the pregnancy developed, her anguish at being kept from the exciting games diminished. Smiling contentedly one day, Boudica decided that she had everything that a woman could wish for - a loving husband, a baby arriving in time for the spring solstice, and a suite of rooms in Prasutagus's villa for herself and the new child.

When it was due to come, the infant, struggled against being born. After taking all day to make its appearance, the midwife called to Prasutagus to give Boudica a potion to relax her birth path. His knowledge of such medicine was the best in all Britain. He made up a mixture of herbs including the bark of the ash tree and fine tinctures of those plants that given in excess would cause the sleep of death, but in his hands were to give Boudica a short, peaceful slumber.

It was his crafty hands as they massaged her back, which proved prove the best remedy. Prasutagus stroked Boudica's damp forehead with a cloth wrung out with sweet smelling flowers, and whispered endearments and words of encouragement. Then cleverly he moulded the baby in her belly with his large, powerful hands into a position with its head ready to enter the world.

Eventually a daughter, with black curly hair and deep blue eyes, arrived. She gazed about the birth room in the villa before she decided to utter her resentment, then she looked directly at her mother and let out an indignant cry as if to blame her for the difficulty.

Prasutagus emerged from the birth room a triumphant man. He had helped produce a healthy girl child who would be his heir. Boudica in the deep sleep after the enormous labour she had of bringing her first-born into the world, saw only his straight back and joyful step as he left. It was enough to please her that she had made her husband proud.

Later when she awoke to find that she had a baby girl, her happiness was complete. Prasutagus came to pay his respects to a new member of the Iceni tribe and bless the mother, a duty he performed to every mother and child born, with delight!

Now he seemed to be walking on clouds. "My lady, what can I say to you to give you the praise that you so deserve?" He was sympathetic to her efforts to give him this scrap of wonderful life, as his.

"Prasutagus, my lord," Boudica breathed slowly, gaining strength, "I am as pleased as you are with our daughter. What name shall we give her?" She held her head to one side as she questioned him, knowing that he probably had already chosen one.

Do you remember that morning by the pool in the forest?" he asked.

"As if I could ever forget!" She smiled at the secret shared with him.

"In Celtic lore there is a goddess Cavatina who is reputed to have given water the power to heal. I believe that Cavatina would make a good name for our girl child. Would you agree to this, Boudica?"

"Yes, my lord, you are so much wiser than I when it comes to knowing Celtic legend, and I like the name too," she beamed, looking directly into those pale blue eyes, then lowered her lashes to hide her response to the flame of desire that had begun to burn in them.

Chapter 15

Prasutagus's male ego responded strongly to the gleam he had seen in his wife's eye. For her part in the birth of his heir, he gave her a team of jet black horses that he had imported from the deserts of Egypt, to pull her own racing chariot as soon as she was fit to learn to drive it.

Shar was given the task of teaching her, and Boudica proved a good pupil. She loved the horses and their gentle natures even though they stood higher than she at the animals' withers. They seemed to know that they were cherished and came at her first call when they were turned loose to graze in the forest, obeying her every command.

Cavatina as the infant was then called, grew strong and healthy, a merry child who was happiest playing among the brightly coloured flowers with the other children of the town.

One day as Boudica watched Cavatina play with some bright glass beads that a merchant had brought from southern Gaul; a messenger arrived for Prasutagus. He brought a message from the Chief Druid calling him back to Mona to assist with the testing of the new acolytes. He suggested that they make a holiday of the journey now that Cavatina was old enough to be left with her nurses.

The thought of seeing new places intrigued Boudica and she agreed immediately. Mona seemed a whole world away and full of mystery to her. She had often wondered what this school of esoteric learning was like.

With autumn approaching she thought that it might be prudent to take her wolf skin cloak to keep out the evening chill, but when she looked in the room of robes, it was not there. True, she had hardly worn it since Cavatina was conceived and she had not searched it for moult. It should still be on the special hanger that had been made for it, where the shoulders were padded to keep its shape and tall enough to make certain that it cleared the floor.

"My lord, my wolf skin cloak, I cannot find it!" she all but demanded of Prasutagus.

"Wife, do you think that I have stolen your precious cloak?" he replied. He had now become accustomed to Boudica's haughty manner, and did not mind it, knowing that she would be contrite once she knew where her cloak was.

"The summer brings with it vermin that would attack your cloak. There is a place where deep holes are dug to get the flint stones; and it is too cold for moths and other burrowing creatures that would make a meal of your cloak. I had it taken there with a little surprise that I was keeping for you." True to his knowledge of his wife, she coloured at her shame of even thinking that Prasutagus would destroy her favourite cloak.

"Come my beloved, let us go and search out this flint mine and discover what it is that I am hiding from you." Prasutagus's eyes glinted with merriment. He was obviously enjoying Boudica's discomfiture as together they walked to the stables where the groom was already waiting with Prasutagus's favourite racing chariot. Shar and some pack ponies were also ready with provisions for many days.

Boudica turned to face Prasutagus. "You knew that I would ask for it!" Boudica snapped at him. She could feel her temper getting out of control.

"Yes wife, I knew and now let us go to the mines and have no more of your rage. We will discuss our expedition to Mona as we go." He added as an afterthought, "With your cloak."

Prasutagus knew that he should not have uttered that jibe but it was apparent that he loved to see the heightened colour in Boudica's cheeks when she was angry.

She glared at him, her eyes sparkling, but she knew not to say anything further on the matter. Prasutagus was no fool and could easily tie her brain in knots with his arguments. She would get her own back at some time. She would pounce when he had forgotten this squabble.

Prasutagus had wrapped his sinewy long arms around Boudica as he held the reins in his enormous hands. She stood safe and secure in the jolting chariot. She knew that in his arms she would always be protected, yet there were times, without any reason, that she sensed all was not well. A sneaking premonition would invade her feeling of happiness. It came from deep within her mind and could not be recognised.

Perhaps it was the concern of another child; it was always wise for a monarch to have more than one offspring in case the first one was taken from them by sickness or accident. Yet Prasutagus had made no attempt to pursue this need.

Boudica mused on this, and on the fact that they had recently had more than one argument. I am getting complacent and bored. Cavatina no longer needs my milk. She plays happily with other children and her nurses. It's time I had another baby to care for; mother had one every year, but I suppose that Prasutagus's age makes it impossible for him to produce seed. Wondering if this was why he had been away so much of late, she felt sad and tried to think of ways of helping him feel confident enough at least to attempt to place his seed in her again.

As they made their way across the autumn landscape, Boudica noticed that the trees were bare of leaves, berries had been picked clean and grass had turned a dark golden colour.

"Winter will be early this year and cold, don't you think my husband?" she asked him.

"Why do you say that, Boudica?"

"Look. Everywhere there is the sign that Andraste is gathering her stores to feed her wild animals through the long nights of ice and snow.

"The leaves and wild fruit have gone from the hedgerows, only the ivy and purple sloes remain. The

65

wild pigs forage for acorns until their stomachs are bulging full!" Glancing up, she pointed at the sunset sky. "And see, the winter geese are already flying to our water meadows; they should not be here for several days."

Prasutagus laughed joyfully. "All this you have learned in a few years, Boudica. I wonder what else you have learned since you came to Iceni?" He looked down at his wife cradled in his arms with a gaze so deep that it penetrated her skull, searching for…what?

After scrutinising her face carefully, Prasutagus whipped the horses lightly to a gallop. "There is a place that we should visit before we go and find your cloak, Boudica. It's a very pretty place full of deer and even in the depths of winter, water runs freely from an underground spring." Prasutagus seemed to be in an excellent mood as if he were enjoying an amusing story that only he knew about.

Chapter 16

He's planning something, and I hope that I too can find mirth in his surprise, as he seems to think that I will, thought Boudica. She had found that not all of Prasutagus's surprises had been pleasant. There had been the time when he had been gone on a journey far away, beyond the Middle Sea, and had come home to Iceni Venta sooner than every one had expected. He had brought some gifts with him then for her and Cavatina. Upon opening the carefully wrapped package, they had discovered the skins of venomous snakes that had curious markings on their heads.

Boudica remembered that she had snatched the skins from Cavatina's plump little fingers, screaming at Prasutagus, "Don't you know that snakes can still bite you even though they be dead?"

"Wife, these snakes have been dead for months!" he had explained.

"I still don't like it. My younger brother was bitten by a snake that Sven had beaten to death, and my mother would never allow a snake dead or alive in the home again."

Prasutagus's face had been an image of mystery. His eyes had rested upon her as if he were seeing her for the very first time, and he had quietly taken the offending skins away.

When he returned, it was as if nothing unpleasant had taken place. Prasutagus was all smiles as he sat down on a sofa upholstered in gold brocade that he had brought home from one of his trips. He picked Cavatina up onto his lap to play with the jewelled pin that Boudica had presented to him on their wedding day.

"The little lady likes exciting jewels, my love. We will look among our treasure chests to find something to make up for my error of judgement with the skins." He glanced up at Boudica to see what her reaction was.

"My lord, Cavatina is not yet of age to care much for valuable trinkets, perhaps you would like to consider the day when she is of an age to be a woman, and then you might want to give her something of value then?"

"Ah, wife, once again you read my mind. The gold miners of Ordovise and Silures are even now gathering enough gold to make our daughter her first torque."

As they headed west towards the setting sun, the landscape was covered mostly with oak interspersed with elm and alder. Occasionally they would encounter large herds of deer that ran off after they realised that the horses were accompanied by their deadly foe - man!

"Where will we be sleeping tonight my lord?" Boudica asked as they passed through a thicket that still had dark sloes hanging from the thorny branches.

"First, we go to the settlement of Dere Well, where we are expected. There will be feasting, with plenty of wine and mead. The good wives will have made bread and cakes for us; it's a happy place where food is abundant and the children grow strong and healthy."

"It seems that we will be having a cheerful night, my lord."

"Yes! But first we will bathe in the deep pools that are fed by a spring that can cure most ills. The water is cold for it comes from a bottomless pit in the bosom of the earth, but it never freezes, even in the depths of the coldest winter."

"Are you ill then, my lord?"

"No!" he replied, "but you will find the water very refreshing after the long drive."

Boudica sensed an ambiguity. Prasutagus has a surprise waiting for me, so he said. Now he wants me to bathe in ice-cold water when we have a hot bath in the villa? My patience is being stretched to the limit, she fumed to herself.

Dusk had fallen as they entered the compound where some blazing hot fires were roasting oxen, boars and deer.

Boudica decided that it was indeed a pleasant place as music from harps, flutes and drums wafted on the air. There was a young man singing a plaintive love song about a lover who had left his lady in search of adventure and wealth. While he was away, his lady had died of a broken heart and when he returned he found her resting place among the flowers. The song ended and the evening seemed to be haunted by the melody.

The headman came and greeted Prasutagus and Boudica before taking them to a roundhouse where everything was supplied for all the needs of the two guests. Two long woollen cloaks lay beside soft sandals. As soon as they had taken off their travel-stained clothes and put on the robes and sandals left for them, Boudica and Prasutagus were led to a large pool with an oval bubbling well at its side.

Prasutagus dropped his cloak and stepped carefully into the well's perimeter. "Is the water very deep, my lord?" she asked.

"The centre of the well is bottomless. No one knows for certain how deep the well really is: You can walk in safely at the edge of the pool though." Prasutagus indicated to where a flight of oak log steps had been laid in the surrounding sandy soil leading down to the water's edge.

Boudica looked about her. The rush lights that had been lit as they had approached the well, flickered brightly, and she could see that apart from her husband, it seemed as if there were only their waiting servants watching; so she too kicked off the sandals, dropped the woollen cloak and dived head first into the centre of the well, the black water closing over her head.

Down, down, into the icy, mysterious darkness. What a relief! Alone in the depths of dim shadows with a current of water gently trying to lift her up to the surface, the underground stream slid over and caressed her tired limbs. She felt as if she could linger in its depths forever. She looked about her to see in the dim shadows that the sides of the well were of jagged rock and nothing like the surface soil. The water tasted bitter with something that was unfamiliar to her. At first she puzzled about the taste then decided that it must be the reason Prasutagus had said that the well had healing properties. Whatever it was, Boudica decided that if it made Prasutagus feel vigorous, then it would be worthwhile coming to Dere Well, and not just because of the friendly nature of its inhabitants.

The pain in her breast warned her that soon she must breathe or die and so surrendering to the demands of her body, she surfaced for air. Like a cloud of red seaweed, her hair floated about her that became a cape protecting her breasts as she raised herself from the water.

She became aware that she and Prasutagus were no longer alone. Many of the people from the settlement stood around the pool were gaping at her! It was if they had never seen a woman take a swim before.

"Come, my lady, there is a warm fire and a drink of hot mead awaiting you, for you must be frozen as the snows in winter." A serving maid was holding out the warm cloak for her.

"Oh, but that was wonderful! I must come here again to swim, for the water is as refreshing as the seas at home!"

"My lady, you were under the water for too long. We all thought that you had drowned. We keep the well covered at all times except when the children are asleep, for it has been known for one of them to stray and fall in, never to surface again." The touch of her hand was that of concern and in the rush lights, her eyes were sorrowful.

Chapter 17

"The child's mother - her heart must have been pierced by the pain of her loss."

"Indeed it was," and a tear of diamond clarity spilled from the dark eyes to trickle down her gentle face.

"Tell me, by what name are you known?" Boudica asked.

"Fililpenda, my lady," she replied.

"Fililpenda, I will see you before I leave."

Later the people were all waiting for their guests of honour as Prasutagus and Boudica stepped from the roundhouse. They were now dressed in brightly coloured robes that gave them comfort and warmth against the coming night, for the feast would last for many hours.

The large meeting hall where council and judgement of disputes were held had been laid out with trestle tables and chairs. Rush lights and oil lamps had been lit to give it an ambience of warm, cheerful friendliness.

Boudica looked about the room and realised that these people whom she had never met before, had done everything possible to make her stay a joyful one.

"These are good, kind people," she told Prasutagus as the dawn came over the horizon and finally they had they made their way to their beds.

Before they left to continue their journey the next day, Prasutagus gave council to an argument that had arisen over the distribution of the free game-meat that had been caught by the hunters that Shar and the other men that Prasutagus had as an escort.

Boudica waited for him in the comfort of the house that had been allotted to them. She sat and thought about the woman who had lost a child to the well, and wondered how it could have happened that it should drown when the stream that fed it had pushed her to the surface.

There came a light scratching at the doorpost. Her serving maid went to answer it. Fililpenda had come to see her.

"My lady, our wise woman Betulanter would speak with you, if you are pleased to go to her home?"

Boudica looked up at her. She was intrigued by the summons, for the woman was obviously nervous. What could be causing Fililpenda such concern?

Boudica rose and came towards her. "I would be honoured to meet your wise one. Please take me to her." It would help pass away the time while Prasutagus listened to the points of view put to him by the complainers.

Fililpenda led her to a small round hut at the edge of the settlement, scratched on the door lintel and waited.

The heavy hide covering over the entrance was pulled aside to reveal a neat, sweet smelling though somewhat dark interior with only a brazier to shed light.

The woman who sat in a comfortable chair was so old that her cheeks were sunken through lack of teeth and her eyes were lost in folds of loose skin. Her gnarled hands rested on her lap, and although it would seem that she was blind, she raised a hand as soon as Boudica entered.

"Come in, my lady; this is a great honour that you do our settlement," she croaked.

"It is you who honour me, old mother," Boudica replied softly.

"Come closer, for I have much to tell you and there is not a great amount of time, for you are on a longer journey than you realize."

Boudica edged forward. A seat was placed for her beside the old woman.

"I have been told that you are tall, with flaming red hair, that your given name is Boudica...Victory. Is that so? And is it also true the water bore you up and made no attempt to take you into its depths?"

"Yes, that is so."

72

"There is a lot of toil for you to do before you return to the gods and only you can do it, so you cannot die yet. Tell me, you have but one child a daughter, Cavatina?" Before Boudica could agree, the old crone continued, "There is to be another child, a girl who will fight like a man. Your name was chosen for you to ensure that the battles that you are going to lead will end in victory. Ah, you did not know about your birth star." A cackle of mirth escaped the shrunken lips. "The god of war shone far too brightly and the sky turned red with his fire, and the sky turned green at sunset on the night that you entered this world, my queen," Betulanter muttered under her breath. It seemed as if she were trying to make up her mind whether or not to tell Boudica something that was very unpleasant.

She sighed deeply. "It is your destiny to be our queen and lead a great army in our favour. You married our king even though he was a very old man and he suffers from that poisonous weed, jealousy. You take care not to give him cause, my lady." She seemed to muse over her next words. "It will be this jealousy that will make him say dreadful words to you. However, in his heart he loves you almost too much." Betulanter nodded to herself as she continued to think of what she had said and again she sighed deeply. "I can advise you no more. You must tread the path that was beaten for you before you were even born and no-one can walk it for you or for your children." It seemed to Boudica that Betulanter could tell her more, but decided not to divulge further secrets. "Go with the blessings of the earth goddess, Andraste, for you serve her well, my child." With that the old woman waved a hand to indicate that Boudica should now leave.

Boudica bowed to Betulanter and went back to the lodging house with Fililpenda.

"Your wise woman makes me think that I am to have a hard life, yet Prasutagus has done everything to make my home with him as his wife, a happy one," she said to Fililpenda.

73

"Whatever Betulanter says, is true my lady, for she sees deep into everyone's heart who enters her home. She has told me that she will always tell the truth on pain of death," was the servant's reply, and then they walked in silence for the rest of the way back to the guesthouse.

Next morning Boudica sought out the maid Fililpenda who had placed the woollen cloak about her shoulders as she had emerged from the well and later escorted her to Betulanter's hut.

Boudica proffered a small ring of silver chaste with gold. "I have only one child, my daughter Cavatina," she said as she placed the ring in her hand, "and I know that I would gladly surrender my life for hers. This is a small gift from one mother to another. If ever you or I need a friend, we will call upon the other. I will not fail you."

"Nor I you, my lady," and Fililpenda gave Boudica the headband that she wore to hold her dark curly hair in place. "If the need arises send this to me and I will come at once, my lady."

Queen and serving maid looked at each other. Neither could explain the bond that held them together, yet both knew that it would never be broken and would be called upon at a time of great distress. They parted, not knowing if they would ever need the bond that they had made.

Shar had prepared all the travelling chariots for them as Prasutagus emerged from the council meeting. The horses were fresh from a night's rest and were anxious to be away, snorting, stamping their feet and flicking their long tails.

Chapter 18

Prasutagus's chariot led the way from the settlement amid cheerful cries of farewell. They headed west on the track toward the Roman road that led to Ratae Coritanorgrum. As they approached the new road, Prasutagus held up his spear to direct them to follow him and he ordered Shar to keep the entire group close.

The setting sun was still in their faces when Prasutagus called a halt for the night and instructed Shar to make camp, light fires and collect some game to roast.

The chariots were pulled from the Roman road and formed a circle in a coppice of hazel trees. There were plenty of nuts lying about and as soon as Boudica descended from the chariot, she started collecting them, glad of the chance to exercise. Bending over and gleaning the treasure of the woods, she became aware that someone was watching. A twig snapped. "Who is there?" she called out but no one answered. Disconcerted, she made her way back to where Prasutagus sat on a stool that Shar had unloaded for him, and attempted to tell him of her fear that a miscreant was observing them but Prasutagus's attention was focussed on overseeing the preparations for the night and the care of the horses.

The busy servants erected leather tents and soon had a grand blaze going. Some boar and eating fowl had been set to cook and soon the air was redolent of the savoury odours of roast meat.

As Boudica sat beside Prasutagus on the leather and fur rugs to eat the evening meal, she shivered and held the woollen cloak that he had given her, tightly about her shoulders. Cold winds stirred the wattle and reeds that grew in profusion in the thicket.

The hot tender meat had been flavoured with root vegetables, and she held her dish to warm her hands. Her stomach rumbled with anticipation as she bit into the juicy cut that Shar had selected for her. He had taken care that his king and queen were given those joints that they preferred and made certain that it was cooked the way that they liked best. Honeyed wine and bread made the ordinary meal a feast.

Prasutagus seemed to enjoy the rough life of travelling and was in high spirits. He unslung his harp from his shoulder as soon as he had filled his empty stomach. His song about a wandering tinker who mended pots and broken hearts, caused laughter at the ribald insinuations.

While he sang, Boudica called Shar to her side. "Shar, while I was picking the hazelnuts, I think I heard someone in the dense bushes and I felt as if I were being watched."

Shar closed his eyes as he thought and when he opened them he said, "Do not concern yourself, my lady, I will search the woods. Also I will keep watch this night. No one will disturb my Lord or you this night." He blinked his dark brown eyes and added as an after thought, "There is no need to inform my master of what you have told me. It would only cause him unnecessary worry." He nodded his obeisance to Boudica, and turned his attention to his duties.

Boudica knew that Shar would guard them with his life and even surrender it if required. It was then she realized that she loved this man like a brother.

The night passed without incident and next morning, everyone refreshed themselves with hot mead and bread. Boudica went into the thickest part of the coppice with a serving maid to relieve herself. She knew that in spite of Shar's careful guardianship, she could take no chances and allow herself to become prey to some wandering vagabond intent on mischief. However there seemed to be no trace of anyone hiding, and they went back to where her husband was waiting for her.

Prasutagus commanded the army of servants and guard-hunters to face south and told them they would not be halting until the sun was well past the noontide.

Grateful for the comfort trip into the woods, Boudica climbed up into Prasutagus's chariot with a smile playing about her lips.

"You are pleased, my lady?" he asked her.

"Indeed, husband. I am happy to ride as far as you command, though I may become famished. Do we not stop for food?"

"No, everyone can eat as they ride. Where we are going it is best for us to arrive in daylight." His glance was still enigmatic. His behaviour had been unfathomable since they had left the villa in Iceni and as much as Boudica liked surprises, she hated not being party to a secret. In truth, she was feeling piqued.

Prasutagus had looked at her as if to ascertain her reaction to his orders, but he said nothing further, and Boudica had to content herself with his manner.

The chariot jolted over the cobblestones and hard-packed earth laid down by the Romans. By the time Prasutagus called a halt, she was aching in every limb. Would there be a well of cool water waiting for her at this place, she wondered?

Prasutagus directed them to stop in a quiet glade clear of the main road, where marching soldiers frequently passed them, heading north.

Boudica eased her stiffened knees to get down from the instrument of torture. She felt as if she never wanted to mount the chariot again...not ever!

Prasutagus grinned. The merriment in his eyes told her that he knew of her discomfort. "Come my beloved, there is a lake nearby for you to swim and food is already caught for the roasting or the pot." Boudica knew that he was secretly laughing at her distress, although he felt compassion for her.

"In this place we have an ancient mine where once they dug out flint stones that were prized as arrow heads. There are deep and dangerous shafts around, and so you need to place your feet carefully, my lady." His grim expression relaxed into a smile as he then said, "They are hard-working and kindly people. I'm certain you will find them to your liking."

Chapter 19

True to his word, people from the nearby settlement came to greet them and a woman led her to where a stream fed a placid lake of azure blue. A sigh of relief escaped her as she started to take off her travel stained clothes. Her own maid helped her to undo the knot that held her girdle tightly to her shift and kept it above her knees while they travelled. Then she removed the hardwearing, boiled leather sandals that Prasutagus had suggested she wear for this journey, as they were so much heavier and unyielding than the soft kidskin ones she wore in the villa.

The lake beckoned and without looking to make certain that the maids and she were alone, Boudica threw off her shift and waded in. The water was much warmer than she had expected, almost like taking a bath at the villa. When it reached her chin, she dived into the depths.

She was elated to see fish swimming with her. Plump trout and schools of sticklebacks came and inspected her. A sudden movement caught her eye and as she glanced down, a shadow the size of a full-grown stag, stirred, and a trout nearly as her long as her extended arm, disappeared into the jaws of a hideous fish. The teeth were long, white and very sharp. Boudica had seen such a monster only once when her brother Sven had brought one home from a fishing trip. He had said it had been caught while they were trawling for cod. The man-eater had bitten a trawler-man in half as it was brought on board.

But that was a sea fish, and this was a lake of fresh water, she reasoned. Its wide, flat head moved from side to side searching for prey. It turned its baleful attention to her. Its dead grey eyes were without mercy and it would attack her and tear her to shreds given the opportunity. Gradually it inched its way closer to her. She was held spellbound, but her subconscious was telling her that she must defend herself somehow. To kick for the surface would mean that the fish would grab her by the legs and drag her to her death. She had no option; she had to face this monstrous devil.

Everything that Sven had taught her about self-defence flashed through her mind, but nothing seemed to fit this particular emergency. Then she remembered the ploy of gouging out an opponent's eyes with her thumbnails. She felt for the bottom of the pool with her feet and entrenched them firmly to give stability when it struck. Then she bunched her hands into fists, the thumbnails protruding over her knuckles, and waited.

Lazily the nightmare swam towards her. You have never had your prey retaliate before, so this will be a little shock for you, she thought. The hideous maw opened, ready to snap shut on her shoulder. While the beast concentrated on where to sink its teeth for the best morsel, Boudica thrust the pointed nail of her right hand deep within its eye socket. The tough, resilient covering gave way, sending the creature into a frenzy of lashing and writhing pain.

Not waiting to watch what it would do next, Boudica barrelled her body to the surface. She shot into the open air and gulped the life giving oxygen. She swam to where her maid was waiting with a drying cloth and woollen cape, and for a few moments she stood completely bare of clothing, trembling.

Once more she felt eyes upon her, eyes that she sensed were dangerous and even more treacherous than the horror that she had just encountered in the pool. An ice-cold toad of fear squirmed its way down her spine, as she searched the surrounding undergrowth for an intruder, but nothing moved; no shadow was deeper than any other. All was silent and still. Perhaps I am imagining it because I am far from home, she reflected.

The woman from the settlement led Boudica and her maid to a flint stone house. Its floor of beaten earth was covered with rushes and the woman indicated this was for her use. Inside, fresh clothing had been laid out and a flagon of mead stood on a table beside a rough, earthenware cup moulded from clay and then baked.

Prasutagus came in and asked her if she was now fit company for the people who lived here.

"Yes, my lord. The lake was wonderful, even warm, thank you! I feel well enough to meet these subjects of ours, and if they are only partly like those at Dere Well, then I think that I shall be pleased to do so." She smiled and with a cup of strengthening mead inside her and clean clothes, she was feeling so much better than she had on her arrival. Her spirits lifted enough to make her want to laugh. "Perhaps they will tell me about the monster that dwells in the blue lake, for I have just met it and have given it something to think about before it tries to take a sample of my body again." She walked with a swing of her hips and gave a skip from time to time. The confrontation with the gigantic fish had made her pulses throb with excitement and for a while she had felt really alive.

"My love, what are you saying?" Prasutagus asked.

"I am telling you that there is a fish in that lake as big as a stag, and it likes to eat people!"

"Impossible." His eyes opened so wide, Boudica thought that they would leave their sockets.

"Prasutagus, I have seen fish like it before, but they belonged to the sea, and they do indeed eat people."

"Come, we will talk to Uriticor the head man here and find out more about this monster." Prasutagus grabbed his wife's arm. His strides were the longest that Boudica had ever seen him take, and he almost dragged her to where a much larger flint house stood.

"Uriticor," he called out, "are you there?" An elderly man appeared at the doorway, his face full of fear as he met Prasutagus.

81

"My queen tells me there is a giant, man-eating fish in your lake, and she has confronted it. What do you know of it?"

Uriticor came from his house and looked so bewildered that Boudica felt a tremor of laughter shake her ribs. He fell to his knees and declared that he knew nothing of it, for never would he put his queen in jeopardy.

Prasutagus looked down at the man who was grovelling at his feet. "Get up man! Nothing can be gained by snivelling." Boudica had never seen her husband so angry. His face was the colour of ox liver and his huge hands balled into fists.

"It must be new to your lake, so how did it get there?"

Uriticor got up on trembling knees. Tears ran down his old, lined face and the misery he felt having caused Boudica to almost lose her life made him look a picture of despair.

"My lord, there was heavy rain some days ago. The river overflowed its banks and the lake was joined to those big ones in the forest. That is the only place it could have come from." Uriticor looked hopefully at Prasutagus, wondering if this reason would be accepted.

"Yes, you could be right. The next thing is, how are we going to put an end to its mischief?"

Boudica, at last could hold her mirth no longer and laughed aloud. Then still with a broad grin, told them, "It is simple. My brother and his friends trawled for fish with nets. We can do the same with the pond. Stretch a net across the pond and drag it from one end to the other."

Both men turned to look at a woman who knew more than they did about this problem and how to solve it. Their eyebrows were arched and a smile played about Prasutagus's face.

Chapter 20

"So, my lady, you wound the fish, escape from its jaws, then you inform us how to destroy it. Is such the way of an Iceni queen?" His smile was one of inquiry.

"My lord, how would you have me for your queen?"

Boudica kept her face without expression. Prasutagus would not answer the question. This she knew; or else he would tell a half-truth. The complete truth was something that she was aware would never be disclosed to her or any other living being because Prasutagus had never admitted it to himself why he had married her, a young healthy woman from an alien country, as a last resort to obtain an heir to his kingdom and nothing more. If now he really did love her, it was because he had become accustomed to her presence in his villa and also in his bed. Boudica hated being told lies and so she never asked his reasons for choosing her as his wife.

"First we will eat. We have travelled the length of the Roman road with very little sustenance. What can your people prepare for us this night, Uriticor?" Prasutagus's hand was still holding Boudica's arm. He tightened his grip and stared down at her. Not waiting for Uriticor's reply he gritted his teeth as he said, "Lady, in future, you do not enter any water outside the villa before it has been searched for such as the thing that you encountered this day, I have never curtailed your activities until now. You will do as I bid. Always a guard will inspect the water. Then and only then, if it is safe, will you enter. I am your king and you will obey me in this matter." He pursed his lips, glaring at her, daring her to retaliate and argue.

Meekly she replied that she would do as he had bidden, with her head hung low so that he would not see the hidden mirth in her eyes. If only my lord knew how well my brother, Sven taught me to protect myself, she mused. Then Boudica asked silently of her favourite goddess Andraste, what is my husband so upset about?

The evening meal was attended by all the work force of the settlement. Men who laboured in the mines and women who knapped the flints into shape, children who searched the woods for provender of nuts and berries, sat about the little flint homes in the clearing, whilst a trestle table had been set up in the long house, used again by presiding councils the same as it had been in Dere Well.

Boudica sat at ease. Prasutagus had opened a precious ampoule of wine and supplied the oil with which the roasting deer and sheep were basted. Aromatic herbs of thyme and chives, which had been introduced into Britain by the Romans, had been wrapped around the carcasses to impart extra flavour. The flames spluttered with the dripping fat and oil and as the warmth reached out to her, she felt lethargic.

The day had been so crowded with activity and had ended with a battle for her life with a huge fish. Prasutagus's anger because she had been careless for her safety. It was all too much. I will definitely have my say if this journey proves to be nothing more than chasing after clouds: He has promised me my cloak and a surprise, and all I have had so far is anger and ill tempered commands! Boudica mused and sipped her wine. When it arrived, the food was a welcome diversion from her thoughts, and she ate greedily, with Shar keeping her platter and wine goblet, filled.

With her stomach full again, Boudica felt as if she could fall asleep where she sat. She laid a hand on that of Prasutagus and told him of her weariness. "You retire now wife. I will join you after I have discussed some matters with Uriticor." His face had lost the stern, uncompromising look that he had shown earlier. He is king and he probably feels that I, as his queen, must take care not to cause more problems than these hardworking people already have, she thought as she rose to go to the lodgings prepared for them.

Then a thought struck her. "My lord, there is something I do not understand. Why are these people still digging up flints when we have good iron tips to our arrows now?" A slight frown had creased her brow as she looked to him for an answer.

"Yes, there is iron for knives and other cutting tools including arrows, but flint makes very good walls if you need to build a really strong house. Using some of the cement that the Romans make, and layering it between the flint, makes a sturdy home that no wind or flood can demolish." His eyes on her, Boudica felt their probe. Prasutagus seemed to delve deep inside her brain and she could find no reason for his scrutiny. She went to her bed still puzzled about it.

Sleep claimed her as soon as her head touched the soft, goose down pillows and Prasutagus's entrance failed to disturb her.

At the break of day, dressed in a pale blue shift and the deep purple woollen cloak that Prasutagus had given her whilst she was without her wolf skin, she greeted the misty autumn morning. The sun, a deep red ball of haze, lifted from beyond the trees surrounding the settlement and cast soft shadows among the huts. Cooking fires sent scented wood smoke curling up into the still air, reminding Boudica that she had not yet broken her fast.

After the meal of warm mead and bread, Boudica realised that Prasutagus had already eaten and was calling to Uriticor for the service of some men to assist him.

Then he turned and welcomed her to the new day. "Come Boudica, I have much to do this day and already the sun is climbing the heavens."

"Where are we going, my lord?"

Without replying he walked to where his guard, Shar stood by his horse, feeding and grooming it.

"Shar, bring some rush lights," Prasutagus commanded his bodyguard.

"Yes, my lord." Shar ran to where a stock of the torches of rush and pitch were housed ready for use, in a dry store and brought four back with him that he had ignited from the cooking fire.

"This way." Prasutagus beckoned to both Boudica and Shar to follow him as he made his way from the centre of the village, to where a tripod of stout timbers squatted over a hole in the ground. A thick rope attached to a winding wheel similar to that used to draw up water from a deep well, was suspended from it into the depths of an underground cave.

"Now wife, let us discover just how brave you are. Your precious wolf-skin cloak is at the bottom of this shaft. Dare you go down after it?"

"My husband forbids me to swim in a lake that *might* have a carnivorous fish in it, yet he taunts me to test my courage over a deep hole in the ground?" She held her head to one side, with a searching, brief look in her eyes, questioning his logic.

Prasutagus gave her a gaze that displayed no annoyance, but surprise. It seemed that he was discovering something of Boudica's personality that he had not known before, and was storing the knowledge for future reference.

Chapter 21

He called the workmen who had been assigned to him by Uriticor. They were dressed in soft leather aprons that were scuffed with white chalk. Their hands were broad and coarse, their nails broken, the mark of hard manual labour.

"Shar, lead the way. You men will lower him down. Carefully mind!" he commanded.

The workmen scurried to do the king's commands. Shar sat in a loop of rope upon which a flat piece of wood had been placed to make the bare rope seat more comfortable.

Slowly, Shar disappeared from sight, taking two of the torches with him, and his voice echoed up to them when he reached the bottom.

"Now you, Boudica." Prasutagus held the crude seat steady for her as she eased herself into the precarious loop. She smiled up at her husband and gave him a cheery wave of her hand. "Come my love, let us explore the depths of Andraste's kingdom together," and he gave a nod to the workmen to lower her into the cave.

The walls of the shaft were uneven and knapped flint interspersed with chalk made up the main fabric. Shar waited patiently for her with the torches held high so that she arrived at the foot in flickering light.

Easing herself out of the seat with Shar's assistance, she stood aside and waited for Prasutagus to join them. The sound of iron hammers hitting the flint stone rumbled through the tunnel. There was a chill breeze blowing from another shaft that had been dug to carry the clean air to the miners.

Boudica shivered as she waited for her husband and looked up to see his form filling the channel. He was a big man and the ropes creaked as he descended. She wondered if it was safe for him to hazard this journey into

Andraste's bowels. However he was ready to disentangle himself from the ropes even before he had set foot to ground, taking care to keep the rush lights from burning the sling seat.

"This way," he said and with his head bowed to keep it from hitting the roof of the cave, he led the way down a passage into a gloom darker than any night. Prasutagus seemed to know exactly where he was going and strode with certainty to where a wall of chalk and flint mix, barred his way. He passed the two rush lights that he had carried, to Boudica to hold, then with his knife he stabbed at a chalky face in the obstruction. It crumbled away without any effort, soon there was a hole large enough for him to ease himself through.

Passing the lights back to Prasutagus through the opening, Boudica followed him into an open cave larger than the villa at Iceni Venta. Boudica gasped in wonder. She would never have guessed that such great holes could be underground without it collapsing.

"Not many people know about this place and I am trusting you to keep it secret too." In the flickering light Prasutagus looked more like a demon than a king, and Boudica felt a tremor of apprehension pass though her for the first time in her life. Instinctively she knew that Prasutagus would be unforgiving if she were to make such a terrible mistake as to reveal this underground place. An uncontrolled shiver shook her frame at the thought of what his retribution would be.

He placed the lights in the sconces fixed into the walls and walked to where several barrels and chests stood. He bent over one, then turning to face her again, he said, "Now, you were wanting your wolf-skin cloak, wife. It is here with some other items that you may find interesting." Prasutagus had opened a sweet smelling wooden casket bound with bronze and pulled out the fur and placed it around her trembling shoulders.

"Here, this is some of the wealth of the Iceni, Boudica. This is what our child will inherit." Prasutagus had opened another container. This time it held gold dishes and cups. In another the gold helmet that he had worn at the rising of the summer sun god. With it was a mask consisting of gold set with precious jewels of scintillating green and red.

There were flagons of oil stacked to one side of the cavern with wine ampoules laid beside them. A small casket that Prasutagus had opened for her inspection contained jewels of every hue. They sparkled with all the colours of the rainbow in the dim oily light, like a thousand suns.

A knot of fear gripped Boudica in her stomach. Why was Prasutagus showing her all his riches? She sensed that he was somehow playing a game with her and only he knew the rules. Did he think her avaricious, she wondered? Was this a test of her loyalty to him?

Questions that had no answers assailed her brain. I will keep my patience and wait for him to disclose his intentions when he is ready. For now he must be uncertain of what I feel for him and his kingdom, even though I have given him his heir, though something or someone must have given him cause to be so suspicious and it certainly is not me. The wise woman at Dere Well was right. He does feel insecure of his ability to hold my love and allegiance, but who awakened it, she wondered?

Boudica laid a gentle hand on his face and asked, "Is my lord feeling fatigued after the long journey? Let us go to the surface now that I have my beloved cloak. We can come and explore your treasures tomorrow." Her disinterest in all his wealth would certainly bewilder him. She would rather that he was confused than believe her to be a crow seeking trinkets for her nest.

A flash of anger sharpened his eyes and he gasped as if his heart had missed a beat. "My lady has no interest in the wealth that I have accrued for my kingdom?" His voice was guttural and harsh.

"I am interested in all that you have accomplished, my lord. However I look upon the wealth as a gift from the earth goddess, from whom it came. Also I am aware that given very long and bitter winters, this gold would buy our people food to keep them from starving. Why else have you gathered it?"

"Wife! I am at a loss to know what will please you! The snakeskins I brought back for you, you spurned. The woollen cloak I gave you is not as good as that of your wolf-skin. I offer you the choicest of the jewels in this casket and you ask me if I am tired?" His obvious fury had made his pallid face a mottled purple. "Oh woman, what can I do to please you?" His last words were an anguished plea from his heart.

Caught off guard, Boudica found herself without an answer. Then she gathered her courage and asked him, "Why have you been so irritated since your return from your journey beyond the Middle Sea?" She spoke in a low voice, not wanting him to think that she too was annoyed. Shar's passive face remained as still as ever. Only a glint of amusement was caught in the flickering torch that told her he too had noticed his master's ire.

It was Prasutagus's turn to be caught unaware. Until now, Boudica had been a happy, carefree spirit who never asked any awkward questions, and now she was asking about that which was disturbing him deeper than he had ever been, caused by his care for her.

They stood close together in the fitful glow of the rush lights, her body so warm and youthful, he groaned in agony. His thoughts were in turmoil. He must tell her the truth, because anything else would cause even more trouble when she reasoned out his feelings for her.

"Ah, Boudica, you ask of me that which I do not, as a king, wish to disclose. Yet I shall tell you. While I was away, I knew no restful sleep. Every night you would haunt my dreams. Then one night the dream changed. I saw you in the chariot that I had given you at Cavatina's birth, and you were without me. You were in deadly danger. Wolves were tearing at your flesh. My dream never left me even in the bright day and I had no choice but to return to make certain that you were well." His face was now hidden in shadow. A shuddering sob escaped him, and Boudica could only guess how much moral courage it had taken for him to declare his deep concern for her.

Chapter 22

Eventually Prasutagus looked at his wife and declared, "My lovely lady wife, I love you and my heart would cease to beat if ever you vanished from my life." He had sought and found her hands and held them tightly in his huge ones. "Now it would please me if you were to choose just one jewel and then I will know that I still have your favour."

Boudica's heart thudded in her breast. This was the last thing that she had imagined. Prasutagus cared deeply for her, loved her even. "I will accept a precious stone from you, Prasutagus because I know that to do so will give you pleasure, and I will wear it always to remind me how much I matter to you, and I will never take advantage of your love... I promise!" She looked up at him as she spoke so that there would be no doubt in his mind that she meant what she said.

Prasutagus spread the jewels out on a soft kidskin so that their brilliance and colour were seen clearly in the gloomy cavern. Blue, green, red and purple, gems sparked, pearls reflected their lustre, but it was a stone whose colour reminded her of the ocean in winter, that Boudica chose.

The turquoise nestled between rubies of immense value, yet it was the only gem that she would have. She pointed it out to Prasutagus and asked if she could have it. "Certainly, though there are gems here that are worth so much more."

"Yes I suppose there are, but this one is like the seas beyond the coast of my homeland after a winter storm. Please may I have it?"

Prasutagus picked out the selected one that Boudica had asked for and placed it in a small squirrel skin bag along with a selection of various other smaller gems, then carefully secreted it inside his over shirt. Then he asked, "Would you have it mounted as a brooch my lady?"

"No, I think that I would like it as a pendant and hang it about my neck to nestle between my breasts, where it will feel my heart beat with my love for you." One day, perhaps, Prasutagus would tell her everything that was of sorrow to him, for she knew that there was still something distressing on his mind that he could not yet tell her.

The chill air reminded them that they were deep in the bowels of the earth and should return to the surface. The entrance to the treasure cave was sealed and Shar blocked it with some huge flints stones far too heavy for the mineworkers to lift.

The journey back to the outside world was easy. Workmen heaved on the ropes and once again Boudica breathed fresh air.

The scent of roasting lamb assailed her nostrils as her head rose above the rim of the mineshaft. Her stomach rumbled in anticipation of the hot, tender meat swimming in fat.

She looked at her shift to be certain that it had not been torn or made dirty by the trip down the mine. Her hands had become whitened with the chalk dust and she called her serving maid for some water in which to wash them.

"I would swim, but my lord is adamant. I must never swim unless the pool is proven safe. I do not know how long I will be able to comply with these restrictions, though I will try not to cause him any more grief," she said to the serving woman as she lathered her hands with the soap.

"My lady is becoming wise in the ways of men," she said with a knowing smile. Boudica washed her hands and rinsed the dust from her face with the sweet smelling soap. She felt refreshed though her mind was still on the conversation that had taken place in the mine.

Prasutagus had taken her there for many reasons and not just to collect her cloak; of this she was certain. The revelation about the store of hidden wealth was not a surprise either. Her father had told her that Prasutagus was very wealthy. Mmmm... I need more patience than I possess, for I must wait and discover what is behind all this display of gold and jewels and I do not think the answer is coming in on the next tide. Her thoughts would not be still, but she would keep them to herself, for to ask Prasutagus would only bring half-truths or denials.

With the wolf-skin cloak about her shoulders once more, she went out to find a gathering of people from the mine waiting for the meat to finish cooking.

The mid-day sun was warm on her skin and she lifted her face towards it. Prasutagus interrupted her reverie as he sat down beside her. "I needed you to know where the real wealth of the Iceni is hidden. It will be there for you if ever you need it, Boudica."

"But you will be with me my lord?"

"Perhaps not. You are so much younger than I and it is only wise that I prepare you for what is to come." There was no sadness in his face, only resignation.

"I do not know what I would, or even could do without your help, Prasutagus." Her hand had searched for and found his.

"I am beginning to think that you will, with your inborn good sense, manage very well."

"It grieves me to hear you speak of such a time."

"My sweet child, do not be unhappy for you have given me so much happiness. Now let us join the workers in their mid-day meal, for I am famished."

Although Prasutagus had told her some of the reasons for presenting his prosperity to her, she knew instinctively that he had not told her all.

The autumn sunshine gave the meal an aura of pleasure. As usual Prasutagus seemed to enjoy the food so much more than when they were attending official banquets with Roman dignitaries or other kings and nobility, and he ate with pleasure.

Chapter 23

After a short sleep, Prasutagus called to Uriticor and asked him if his orders for a net to sweep the lake had been carried out.

He was shown a pile of rough hempen rope that had been woven as Boudica had suggested, strong enough to hold a big fish but with holes just large enough to allow small fish to escape and weighted with some of the heavy flint stone to hold it to the bottom of the lake.

The strongest men, including Shar, spread the net across the lake, and slowly walked from one end to the other. Fish of all shapes and sizes came to the surface in an attempt to escape, the smallest sliding through the net to get away. Then suddenly there was a heavy pull so hard that some of the weaker men were pulled from their feet, but they knew that with their king watching, they must not let go, and held on for dear life.

Huge trout, and eels as long as a man's arm, that had been unable to slide free of the swarming fish fighting for their freedom, swam and slithered in panic. The eels wriggled blindly into the waiting small nets of the women who had come to enjoy the prospect of catching a tasty meal.

However it was the great gaping snout of a pike that caused most terror among the smaller fish. Its huge jaws opened and snapped shut on anything within reach. Gradually the heaving nets came towards the lakes edge. The pike, as Boudica had described, was as big as a full-grown deer. With only one baleful eye, the monstrosity looked about for whoever was responsible for his loss of habitat.

It plunged towards the men, dragging the net, but Prasutagus had his great spear with him and thrust it deep within the eye socket where Boudica had gouged out to whatever brain it had. Anger made the pike throw its body at bystanders. Prasutagus held on to his spear, just as the mineworkers had held on bravely to the nets.

Muscles swelled on his arms and neck. He clamped his jaws tightly. His spear was made for battle, long before he was born. It had served every owner in good stead, and he, King of the Iceni was not about to disgrace the spear by surrendering it to a fish.

He pulled, and with an extra heave, Prasutagus, throwing all of his strength behind it, with the spear's end shaft firmly planted between his feet to hold it steady, slung the pike over his head onto the grassy bank. With the spear still impaled in its head, the fish gasped for the water that gave it life. Prasutagus wrenched the spear free and then thrust it with all of his might down again, into the writhing head once more, to skewer it again. A hush settled on the clearing. Gasps of amazement came from all of those who had witnessed this feat by their king.

Boudica stood white faced, unable to utter a word. Her husband had proved himself to be not just a great man but also a man fit to rule. The fish was still threshing about, its teeth a menace to anyone dim-witted enough to get too close.

"My lord, that was a noble thing that you did."

"Not me, beloved; the spear did not snap or slide out of my hands. It is the spear that is brave." He looked at the shaft, the innocent yew wood, supple yet with strength that defied understanding. It would be as loyal to whoever held it as Shar was to him.

Then his glance turned to Boudica. "And what of you, my lady? This fiend of the lake attacked you, and you poked it in the eye with your thumb nail?" It was a question asked with incredulity. "Look at it," he said, pointing in disbelief.

While they had been talking, Shar had taken a massive great flint stone and brought it down on the head of the pike. It trembled in its death throws, its one good eye fixed firmly on Boudica. Then a final tremor ran through its frame before it died.

A collective sigh went through the people gathered about the lake as life was finally extinguished from the largest fish they had ever seen. Its long body lay flaccid and flies began to gather.

"I suggest that you drag this fish to another part of the forest for the crows to feast upon. Pike do not make as good eating as the splendid trout and eels that you have caught this day. I would be appreciative if I could take some with me to save my guard the work of hunting for our supper tonight, and if you put some of the smaller fish back into your pond, you will have a good catch next year too."

Uriticor was on his knees. "My lord, whatever we have is yours. It is we who are indebted to you. You have rid us of a menace that would have emptied our lake of all fish and water fowl, and provided enough fish for us to salt some away for the winter as well as a feast for tonight. We will invite some people who live to the south of us, and we will sing of your deed." He was so happy; tears ran down his lined face in rippling rivers.

"Come, Uriticor, get your men to help load my chariots, for the day is leaving us fast, and we must be on our way back to Icenorum Venta. We have a girl child and I know that my wife is anxious to hold her again, as am I."

With the chariots laden and the fresh caught trout wrapped in burr leaves to keep them cool, the cavalcade set out on its return journey northeast for home.

A joyful greeting welcomed them as they rode into the streets of Icenorum Venta. Little Cavatina was held out for Boudica to take from the child's nurse. Her solemn face broke into a gleeful grin when she realised that her parents had come back for her.

Prasutagus called for the fires to be lit for the hypocausts that warmed the bathing room and water, a hot bath, a nourishing meal of baked suckling pig with some sour apples, then his bed. Boudica knew that he was exhausted and needed to sleep, yet this journey had opened her eyes to the fact that though they had been husband and wife for four years, it was only on this expedition that she had learned anything about the man she was joined to. She needed to talk to him, so during the bath, as she handed him a goblet of wine spiced with nectar, she looked directly into his face to determine if he would be receptive of her questioning. But his eyes were dull and the dark shadows around them brooked no argument. His brain was too fatigued to consider the saga of their marriage and what his plans were for their future.

The evening meal was quiet; Cavatina had been put to sleep in her nurse's room. Prasutagus drank some more wine to quench his thirst caused by the dusty road, then held his arm out for Boudica to join him in their bed.

The travelling chariots hardly seemed to be unpacked from one journey, when they were being made ready for the next that would take them to Mona. Boudica began to realise that this was the kind of life that Prasutagus preferred, always moving, always finding a new horizon.

For the trek from east to west of Britain, Prasutagus had commanded that they leave at daybreak. They would greet the sun god with a song and break their fast then be on the road before the morning star had left the sky.

With the sun on their backs, the cavalcade set out in good speed. The first stop would be for a mid-day snack of bread, dried beef and eggs, with some mead to wash it down. Boudica had made certain that her maids had packed warm shifts and night covers, including the huge skins of the white bear that she had brought with her from her homeland for the frosts of winter had already whitened the hedgerows.

Prasutagus knew the way to Mona well and directed them to where the water was fresh and the game plentiful. They crossed Roman roads but did not travel on them, keeping to the half hidden tracks of vehicles that had gone this way for aeons.

On the third day since they had left Icenorum Venta, Prasutagus called a halt in a wooded glade beside a high hillock. He motioned to Shar, who immediately ran to the hill and with the setting sun, sent a shining message to whoever was watching from the distant tower in the academy. Shar returned and gave Prasutagus a nod and smile. He had done his master's bidding without a word having been spoken. "Rest and water the horses; clean as much of the dust from the chariots as you can, then prepare yourselves for the entry into Mona." They were to enter the compound before darkness had settled.

"Some of you who are not needed can stay outside the Grand Hall and tend the chariots and animals. I will select those who are to come with me, when we arrive."

Boudica could tell by the timbre of his voice that he was excited. This was the place where he had spent his youth and the early part of his adulthood.

Chapter 24

She did not know what to expect. Would everyone be whispering in hushed voices or at prayers? Anxiety began to gnaw at her stomach. Would she disgrace her husband? Then before any more questions could prick at her brain, she was entering a beautiful garden that surrounded an ancient granite building, whose grey walls were a perfect backdrop for the colourful flowers and herbs that had survived the early frosts and grew in great profusion.

Men in brightly coloured clothes were running to greet them. They laughed with exuberance. "Prasutagus! Welcome. You too, Queen Boudica! We have been keeping watch for your signal from the top tower since midday. Come in and rest." All this seemed to be said in one breath by a man with black flowing locks of hair, and a rosy complexion, whose cloak was a green and red tartan. So much for whispers and prayer chanting, thought Boudica.

Prasutagus introduced her formally to Leofing who had officiated at their wedding and who governed the school. His smiling face had completely dispelled any misgivings that she might have had at meeting this learned and knowledgeable man.

The food was of a variety unknown to Boudica. Even the fish were unusual - huge crabs, larger than any caught off the coasts of Icenorum, lobsters too and the prawns were so large that she had difficulty unpeeling them from their shells; cuts of beef so tender, she could not believe that they came from an ordinary beast, and remarked so.

"We take the sweetbreads from a bull calf when it is still a suckling. The steer then grows very quickly to fine edible beef before it has become tough and stringy. I am pleased that you are enjoying your meal."

Boudica had indeed eaten heartily. The small snack taken whilst travelling had been forgotten well before the sun had gone from the evening sky.

Her goblet had been refilled constantly with mead, and the honeyed wine was making her feel drowsy. Her eyelids flickered as Prasutagus emptied his goblet and glanced across to her.

"My lady wearies, and we have a very busy time tomorrow, Leo. So, we'll bid you sleep well this night." He stood up from the dining board and brushed the remnants of food from his tunic, bowed to his host, then held his arm out for Boudica to take.

A young novice escorted them to a room brightly lit with bees wax candles. A large straw filled mattress covered by several sheep fleeces sewn together, waited for them. A serving maid waited for Boudica to help her to unbind her hair and loosen the girdle that had held her shift from above her ankles to make sure she did not stumble on the stone steps leading up to the sleeping rooms. She left when she saw Prasutagus indicate that she should go, as he wished to undress his wife himself.

Prasutagus poured her a small amount of wine while she gazed from the window. Turning to him as he handed her the little silver goblet, she thought, how kind he is to me. She drank the sweet liquor, detecting a slight after taste, vaguely bitter, but she was far too tired to give it any further consideration and fell into a deep sleep as soon as her head touched the soft pillows.

She was aroused at dawn by the sound of a deep toned bell tolling the dawn. Masters and acolytes alike would be outside the school facing the east to welcome the sun god before they broke their fast and commenced the exams and tests for that day.

Prasutagus had already joined them for the morning devotions, and she wondered why he had not roused her. Without waiting for her maids, hastily she rinsed her face free of sleep and put on a clean shift of natural linen.

The sound of the ram's horn echoing from the hills told of the end of worship and time for the breaking of the fast.

Boudica waited for her husband as he strolled towards her. He was talking cheerfully to Leofing, heads together in an intimate conversation that excluded the other masters and scholars. Whatever they are talking about, it's definitely not about the test and exams for the acolytes. This is certainly something very personal to Prasutagus and perhaps his real reason for coming here and bringing me with him, she concluded.

Once the first meal of the day was ended, a hush settled over the School of Learning. Boudica sat with her maids in a sun-warmed corner of the herb gardens and enjoyed the heady perfumes that permeated the air whilst the Chief Druid, Leofing, with the aid of Prasutagus and other Master Druids, gave the young students their tests.

Whilst they prepared her for the evening meal, the eldest of them asked, "Can my lady tell us when we will be returning to Icenorum?"

"I think that my lord is happy to be among his old companions. It will be difficult to pry him away, therefore I suggest that you make yourselves comfortable here." Boudica did not mean to be unhelpful, but she was at a loss. Prasutagus had not told her anything about this mission and she was as ignorant as her servants.

Boudica dressed in a gown of copper coloured sheer, fine silk that Prasutagus had given her for the occasion. The jewel of aquamarine that she had chosen from his treasure, had been mounted in gold and surrounded by small gems of every hue, and hung about her neck to rest between her white, plump breasts. Her dressing maid had tamed the cloud of hair whose colour had not altered since her arrival in Icenorum, enough to accept the circlet of gold that she had worn on her betrothal journey to the Iceni king. She then wove wreaths of thornless rosehips around her head.

The gold torque that Prasutagus had given to her on their wedding day was also around her neck. Boudica looked every inch, Queen of the Iceni, wife of King

Prasutagus. Her proudly held head and straight back proclaimed her so.

Boudica noticed that her dressing maid stood at the top of the steps to watch the reception of her queen by Prasutagus and his compatriots. A smile of conceited contentment played about the woman's face and glinted in her eyes, Boudica smiled in conspiracy with her.

Taking care to avoid tripping on the granite stairs, Boudica descended slowly into the grand hall, where huge copper shields had been placed craftily so as to catch and reflect the evening sunlight, into every corner of the darkening room. Glancing about the great room that lay below her, she noticed everyone had raised their heads to look at her!

The senior Druid priests, Leofing and her husband, were talking among themselves whilst waiting for her.

Most of those assembled were white-haired men and women wearing gay tartan cloaks and even brighter tunics, though some were young and wore plain natural un-dyed tunics tied with flaxen ropes about their waists.

One young man of her own age seemed to be overwhelmed at the sight of her; he gazed in admiration and seemed lost to the world about him, momentarily their eyes met and Junus, as he was called, was cursed to never forget the golden queen of the Icine!

In the hall, a startled hush and held breath brought all conversation to a halt.

Chapter 25

Boudica's eyes were for Prasutagus alone. Leofing and he came to meet her. Prasutagus held out his right hand to take her to be introduced to the company and Leofing took her other hand. Boudica could see she had made an impact on the gathering. Was this what Prasutagus had planned, she wondered? If so, why?

"Leofing, shall we show my Queen the sunset? I doubt if she has ever seen anything like it before. Prasutagus guided her to the doorway that opened out to the western gate just as the sun dipped over the horizon.

A fiery globe dominated the seascape. Reflective clouds of all shades from pale gold to darkest copper surrounded it. The sea was calm; only the smallest ripples hissed and gurgled as the wavelets reached the rocky shore. Shafts of purple, gold, green and blue bounced and twinkled from the serpentine movements. Boudica stood enthralled and motionless at the sight of such a magnificent display.

Prasutagus placed an arm about her waist and whispered, "Come, my love, allow me to show you to the feasting room. I'm certain you are as famished as we are after the long journey we have made this day." His presence broke the spell that bound her to the majesty of the sun god's thrall over her.

The meal was a merry affair with minstrels strumming harps and singing. Sometimes Prasutagus joined in, and then Boudica asked the drummer to keep a pace with her, for she had a song to sing too. She sang in a clear, gentle voice of Prasutagus's kill of the water beast with his spear and how he had thrown it over his head.

Everybody clapped and praised her ingenuity as well as her ability to keep a good tune.

"Yes, it was a good kill, but my wife did not tell you that she had poked its eye out!" Prasutagus said as he laughed aloud.

Later that evening, Prasutagus surprised her by advising her to instruct her maids to pack her warmest clothes in a separate carrier, because they would leave shortly after sun up next morning.

The cavalcade set out as Prasutagus had commanded, Shar leading the way. They came to a valley between two densely wooded hills where the animals were rested and everyone took a break from the difficult terrain.

Bodyguards, servants and Boudica's maids were getting back into their allotted chariots and mounting their horses when Prasutagus gave them the order to proceed to Icenorum without Boudica and him. Only Shar would accompany them from now on.

Boudica was puzzled. What were Prasutagus's plans now, she wondered? It had been three summers since they had journeyed with only Shar for escort and that had been their wedding day. Questions tormented her brain, but she had no answers.

Prasutagus headed south leisurely for a number of days passing through several towns and settlements of both British and Roman occupation. Eventually they came to a small stream. With an imperceptible nod to Shar to make camp, they stopped and dismounted. They were to sleep in an open field!

Boudica could not fathom out what Prasutagus was planning. The nights were very cold; the lady moon was in her first quarter so there would not be much light once the sun had gone from the sky. She was reticent about asking him, for surely he would have told her of his plans if he wanted her to know? What was he hiding from her?

Boudica wrapped her cloak tightly about her. Lowering clouds darkened the sky and a chill wind blew from the north bringing a smattering of icy rain in its wake. Shar was blowing on the fire to encourage it to burn brightly, his round cheeks puffed out by his exertions. He glanced up at her. There was enigmatic cast to his eyes, and it dawned on Boudica that he knew what his master intended. Even though he would give his life to save mine, he will never tell me what Prasutagus plans to do here, she reflected.

Prasutagus had helped Shar to gather kindling; he obviously appreciated and enjoyed the laws of sharing the needs of out of doors life and was glad to be of assistance to help Shar to cook the food. A trap had caught a young deer, which Shar was now skinning, ready to be roasted. Great polar bear skins had been set to warm by the fire.

"My lord, are we to sleep in this open field tonight?" Boudica asked hesitantly. Would he be cross with her for not trusting him?

Prasutagus seemed to think that her question was a jest. "You have no idea where you are wife?" he asked, laughing.

"No, my lord. The low grey clouds and rain have hidden any land marks that I may have seen before."

"You do not recognise where you are Boudica, because we have entered this place from the north west. The last time we were here, we came to it from the south. Now do you know where you are?" Prasutagus was still grinning at her dismay and uncertainty. To soothe her fears he said, "The night is dark my beloved, and you are hungry as well as confused. We will eat and have some wine to warm ourselves then I will lead you to your bed."

Boudica could see that there was still a look of glee on his face. My lord finds something amusing. I trust that I too will be so pleased, she thought.

Full of hot tender meat and wine, Boudica would have been content to curl up in the white bear skins and her cloak and sleep where she sat at her meal beside the fire.

Prasutagus helped her to stand. He carried two of the massive bearskins over his long arms and they walked towards a dark shadow that proved to be a wood. Treading carefully to avoid leaving traces of his passing but making enough noise to warn the night creatures that he was coming, he led her to the glade where they had spent their first night as husband and wife. Then she realised that they were in Seven Snakes Wood!

Prasutagus laid one of the skins on the mossy bank where once he had put his cloak, then placed the other over the top of it, making a snug bed for them.

Boudica let her cloak fall from her shoulders. Prasutagus untied the girdle that held her shift, then he slipped the simple gown from her shoulders too, and Boudica stood marble white in the gloomy woods with only the night animals to watch and see her unclothed.

The pale new moon had not yet risen above the gaunt autumn branches and yet the darkness made Prasutagus appear to be so much younger than he was. He poured wine into two goblets and passed one to her where she stood. A chill ran through her frame. Somehow she felt that this night Prasutagus intended to lay his seed to ripen in her womb. She too wanted another child, yet she still felt uneasy and the tremors made her wine spill over her hand.

Prasutagus took the hand and held it to his lips, licking the spilled wine. "This will be a night that we will always remember Boudica, for I guarantee you another baby will be made." He was now holding her very close. She should be pleased, but the careful planning had made her feel that it was all too contrived to be a child of love.

Chapter 26

She gulped the wine down, shivering with cold and nervousness. Perhaps it would assuage her fears long enough for her to be able to sleep after Prasutagus had given her his seed.

He helped her to the waiting warm, soft furs and taking the empty cup from her, laid her down. His lovemaking was over so swiftly that although the wine had relaxed her, she had not had time to completely respond. He had groaned in ecstasy then relaxed to the point of collapse, flopping on her as lifeless as one of Cavatina's dolls.

This time there was no joyful fulfilment, no violent reaction of her body in answer to Prasutagus, only a yearning for completion. There was none.

Prasutagus was now fast asleep, breathing heavily. Boudica moved from under him and turned to lie on her side to sleep, but even that was denied her.

The moon was now riding high in the starry sky, and pierced the bleak, bare boughs overhead. In the cold night, she felt alone, yet suffocated and badly used.

Carefully she slipped from beneath the bearskin and put her cloak around her. Drawn by her thirst to the sound of rushing water, she made her way to where the waterfall cascaded from the cliff.

The block of granite still stood sentry at the entrance to the secret glade. She took mouthfuls of the clean water to ease her dry throat then sat for a while on the stone block to gather her thoughts. Bringing her knees up under her chin, she rested her cheek on them.

Prasutagus's plans were now as clear as day to her. The beautiful jewels, the gold torque, the magnificent silk gown were not for her, Boudica the woman, but an offering to the sun god and Andraste the earth goddess as an offering for a new child. She was but a vessel for his heir. Prasutagus probably loved her as much as he could love any woman with a young, healthy womb. He was as kind and gentle as any young husband would have been if not more so, and yet...a shiver caused her to tremble and as she thought of returning to the warmth of the bearskin bed beside Prasutagus, she was suddenly aware of watching eyes again. Who could be following her around Britain? And why? In desperation she called out for whoever it was to make themselves known. She knew it was not Prasutagus or Shar. This was that stranger, the watcher in the woods, though no longer a stranger for the prowler had become familiar. She waited, her breath stilled. She called again, and anger was now making her impatient.

A movement in the shadows, and just as Prasutagus had watched from the cover of the boulders and trees, so did this person.

Slowly, a masculine form came out of the gloom, tall, wide of shoulder, upright. In the light of the new moon, she saw his dark skin and close cropped curling hair, a man whose bearing was that of a Roman soldier; his dress as far as Boudica could see, was a dark kilt and short cloak. He did not appear to be carrying any weapons. His magnificent torso was protection enough from any casual assault.

Boudica scrambled to her feet. She would be at a disadvantage sitting on the rock. He came closer, his breath clouding the cold air, and his musky male scent in her nostrils. I should scream for help. Shar would come to my aid, but her voice would not leave her throat. She was without sound, dumb!

Tremors from her toes and the balls of her feet, gradually worked their way up her body until she was shaking and quivering uncontrollably.

Warm hands were stroking her arms and his voice seemed to come from far away. "There is nothing to fear. I could never harm you. You are like the Goddess Aphrodite as she came up out of the sea. I have needed to hold you since I first saw you alight from the long boat that brought you to this cold, dark land."

"You have spied on me all the time I was married to Prasutagus?"

The warmth of his arms and breath were making her feel giddy, as if she had drunk too much wine.

"Most of the time, for I have to obey the orders of the Governor General, and go where he sends me."

So, he *was* a soldier.

His arms had now encircled her waist and drawn her closer; taller than she, he pressed her head into the warmth of his neck. She felt the wolf-skin cloak slip from her shoulders. Once more she was bare of all covering. The trembling would not cease; she wanted to cry, run away, anything but suffer the indignity of having her female flesh respond to this man.

Where was Prasutagus? Why did he have to fall into a stupor and leave her undefended and vulnerable?

Defenceless tears trickled down her face. She felt as if her moon blood was falling, though it should come only at the height of the full moon. If Prasutagus was right, it would be another nine moons before she saw them again, after the birth of a baby.

The moisture descended her inner thighs. Her breathing became difficult as she was held in an embrace of gentle iron strength.

Andraste, help me, she prayed, but the goddess was deaf to her entreaties or else approved of Boudica's predicament, for no one came crashing through the woods to support her.

The fire spread through her body causing agonising pain. Sobbing, finally she capitulated and allowed her head to fall on the stranger's shoulder and surrendered to the demands that engulfed her.

He replaced her warm cloak and scooped her into his powerful arms. He seemed to carry her as lightly as a newborn baby. Water from the falls had carved a pathway

110

through the woods. He ran along it with his treasured burden, unmindful of any vipers or tree roots he could stumble over. Eventually they came into a clearing where a tall grey horse was tethered to a tree and was cropping the shrivelled autumn grass.

He whisked a heavy blanket from the saddle, and spread it on the cold ground. There was a moment when he looked down at her helplessness. He kissed the tears that coursed down her cheeks, and then his lips covered hers. Such a feeling of tenderness overcame her, the likes of which she had never known before. She wanted to hold his head to her breast, and to kiss him in return.

He knelt down on the frozen ground, pulling her with him, and then lying on his back so that the cold did not reach her, he cuddled her on his chest. Unresisting, she proceeded to allow his male member to penetrate where Prasutagus's had failed. And where Prasutagus had been concerned in producing yet another heir, her lover made her feel as if she were the queen of his heart. Deeper into her secret places he thrust, his massive member twice as large as Prasutagus's. She gritted her teeth against what should have been excruciating pain, yet the torture came as unfulfilled pleasure.

Time stood still as wave after wave of agonising ecstasy overpowered her, then she felt as if an iron fist had grabbed her maidenhood and almost squeezed the life out of her.

Her lover gasped, and held her buttocks closer, tighter. He was muttering endearments, telling her how he had fantasized about this moment. Perspiration ran from every pore. He laid her head upon his shoulder again and kissed her. "My dearest love," he whispered, and then heaved a deep sigh.

Chapter 27

This is either a dream or else a nightmare, Boudica thought, for this cannot be real! She knew that she should return to where Prasutagus lay sleeping, but to spend the rest of the night in this man's arms would be worth not being the Queen of the Iceni. But what of her daughter? What of Cavatina? And what if Prasutagus had given her a new baby? Duty to the tribe must come first, just as it did for Prasutagus.

His voice cut through her meanderings. "When you need me again, I will be at your side. Come, I will return you to Prasutagus's side for he is a good king and as much as I would like to keep you for myself, he needs you for his queen."

"Who are you? Where do you come from?" she asked as carefully they picked their way through the woods in the midnight gloom.

"It is safer for you not to know, my Lady Boudica. Britain is changing and a new governor is to be appointed. Now I too must go. Dawn will be over the horizon soon, and I must be at my post. May the gods protect you, Boudica," he said as he bade her, "Sleep well," and kissed her gently on the brow. She wanted to know how would she contact him in times of trouble, but the dark shadows had swallowed him. He had disappeared into the night as silently as he had come. Did he know that this place was the sacred ground of the Druids, she wondered.

As she looked down at her sleeping husband, she wondered if their lovemaking would ever be the same. It would be far wiser for me to forget this night and only think of it as a dream, she mused.

When he awoke, Prasutagus was in high spirits. As they made their way back to Icenorum Venta, tied his horse's reins to Shar's chariot and strummed on his harp.

True to her expectations, she was to have a child at midsummer the following year. Not once did Boudica consider that the stranger could have fathered her child. Prasutagus was her husband and had sown his seeds first. It must be his seed that her womb would accept and no other man's. Anyway, the lover at the waterfall was but an exotic dream, a figment of her imagination nothing more.

To tell Prasutagus that a new baby was on its way was a decision that she put off. He would fuss over her and curtail her freedom. It was as her waist thickened that he glared at her and with his pale blue eyes like flint, he stormed at her, "Now my lady wife, tell me, why do you hide the new life that beats within you?" His eyes searched her face intently for the possibility of deceit.

Boudica sighed. "I knew that you would find out soon enough. You will stifle me with orders not to ride, and not to go out without my maids in attendance, not to swim!" she wailed at him, with anger such as Prasutagus had not seen from her before.

"I am *not* going to pronounce my innocence or deception, if you loved me as you say, then in your heart you will know what is the truth, already!"

Prasutagus looked calculatingly at his wife, trying to decide if she was telling the complete truth. She was right; it was true. He would have halted all those activities that might endanger the unborn child; or was there more to this deception, his sad face asked. He turned from her and left the room with the excuse that he was sleepless, and did not wish to disturb her.

At daybreak when she went out greet to the new morning, Shar was preparing Prasutagus's large chariot and horses for a long journey. Boudica could feel that this was for her husband to get away and reflect on the argument that they had had the evening before. The turmoil in her heart at the thought that Prasutagus no longer loved or needed her, saddened her.

Oh, my lord, if only you had more faith in your own abilities to make me pleased to be your wife, we could be so much happier together. You will return to a child you will recognise as yours alone, she whispered to herself.

Another girl child was born to Boudica after she suffered all the pangs of an uncomfortable pregnancy, with sickness and giddiness at every turn. This child could not be delivered too soon, she thought, for she was tired every waking moment and her ribs felt as if Thor, the god of thunder, had hammered them! This must be a child like no other for length. It will be much like its father and he will never be able to deny his part in its birth.

Several days went by with labour pains a constant companion. Finally the baby emerged late in the evening, after the attending midwife had given up hope of a live child being born that day.

As the shadows lengthened, the cries of a baby could at last be heard. Boudica was delivered of another girl.

The red star of Camulos, the Celtic god of war, was sinking below the skyline, and the brilliant blue-white star, of the heavenly personification of Andraste goddess of the earth, love and life, shone in magnificence overhead. Garian, the headman of the town of Icenorum Venta, took note of this for he was certain that his king would question him about the position of the brightest heavenly bodies.

In place of Prasutagus, Garian came to pay his respects to Boudica and the infant. "My lord Prasutagus should know of his child's appearance, my lady," he said, unhappy that the king was neglecting his queen. "I have commanded that a message should be sent to him for his immediate return!" he said, his head low with embarrassment.

"You know where Prasutagus has gone?" Boudica asked.

"Yes, my lady. He told me that he travels to Mona on the west coast to visit the Druid settlement and halls of learning," Garian replied.

"Can you get a message to him before my baby is walking?" she pleaded.

"Madam, my lord Prasutagus will know by nightfall that he has a new child in his household. I have sent the message by the watch towers, directing the light towards Mona and I've coloured the flames red and gold, those of my lord's cloak!" Garian was pleased that he could help his queen and save his master from what could be a terrible mistake by not acknowledging the new baby as his, for having seen the child himself, Garian knew who the true father was.

Prasutagus arrived before the sun had travelled the sky for three days and slowly came to the side of where the baby should be lying in its cradle. However, a youth bed had been made up for it. The crib was too short for her when she kicked her heels against the ends. Prasutagus had only to glance at this newcomer to know that she was indeed his child.

There lay an exact replica of him, a body so long that the baby cradle was too short just as his had been. She had pale blue eyes and her hands were like a farmer's spade. Her baby feet were long and slender. The infant gurgled and laughed, holding out her tiny arms and she enraptured him. Instantly his heart was hers.

The light that had been missing from Prasutagus' eyes now glowed strangely. Boudica had known that her husband had suspected her of being unfaithful to him. She had realised that words would not heal his doubt and only the proof of his parenthood would achieve belief in her fidelity. The lover in the woods had been lost to her memory as if he had never occurred.

Chapter 28

"You are pleased, my lord?" Boudica asked of him. There was an odd cast to her face that warned Prasutagus to be wary of how he replied.

"Madam, what can a foolish old husband say?" He looked so downcast that Boudica needed to hide the grin that threatened to reveal her pleasure at seeing him so disconcerted.

"So, Prasutagus, you now know that I told you the truth when you questioned me about this child. Believe me now when I tell you that you will only ever hear the truth from me no matter how unpleasant it may be." After telling him this with a cheerless face, Boudica allowed herself to laugh at Prasutagus's discomfort.

"Come my love," she chided him and smiling gaily said, "This misunderstanding has taught us both a lesson. I am headstrong and do not always respect your wisdom, and you must learn to trust me, your wife." She held out her arms to him and he came to her as a lost child to its home. He laid his head on her breasts, and her milk spurted onto his lips, which he tasted with delight. "My wife, your body is as sweet and generous as your spirit!" he said as he glanced up at her through half-closed eyes.

The naming of the new child in Prasutagus's household was a question that would need an answer while the blue-white star reigned supreme in the night sky, for this was the baby's birth star.

"My lady, I do not deserve your affection. However our new daughter deserves the best name that we can give her. While in Mona, we talked about the great healer and priestess Ceridwen, who lived there many years ago. She is still greatly revered by the high priests as a seer, and I can think of no better name for our child. But tell me wife, have you any other name in mind?" He looked at Boudica with such earnestness that she was inclined to smile at his discomfort.

"My lord Prasutagus, husband! Let's not dwell on the past for it helps none. Ceridwen will be our daughter's name. Garian has the place and time of the stars that were in the heavens when she was born, and for what I know of star charts, I think that you have indeed chosen the right name for her, for I feel that she will be a caring child " Boudica felt a sense of relief as they discussed this subject. Prasutagus would now be happy to know that she agreed on the new child's name and let kindness rule his heart, where suspicion had dominated before.

Her father and the rune master had been right, Boudica decided. She had been very happy with Prasutagus, a pale faced man, whose sad, light blue eyes had lit up every time he had seen her, and she in turn had come to love him dearly and smile sympathetically in return, grateful for his obvious adoration of her.

He had taken her to his home in Icenorum Venta, where he had a huge villa that had been built in the Roman manner, with heated floors and walls, which were gaily decorated with fabulous pictures of unheard of animals, in tiny pieces of coloured marble.

There was a heated bathhouse where Prasutagus and she, with their two little girls, would bathe in the luxury of milk warm water that had been scented with oils imported from foreign lands. They used soap that was made by the local women from lanolin, the yellow fat like grease that was made from the leg pits of sheep, wood ash and soda.

The little girls loved to splash and play with Prasutagus and he in turn delighted in their innocence and simplicity. They were a great joy to him as he grew older.

The servants were happy to care for Boudica, going about their work cheerfully, for her mother had taught her that all women were sisters at heart and should be treated as such. They in turn, delighted with her kindness, kept the house spotless.

Prasutagus, an enlightened man, had rebuilt all of his people's homes, replacing the rush-strewn floors, mud and wattle walls, with brick. The villages were clean, well drained, spacious and airy, and illness was rare.

The team of jet-black horses that he had given Boudica as a gift when Cavatina had been born, to pull her own chariot, she had cherished more than any other favour he had bestowed upon her, taking them out for long gallops to neighbouring towns. There were times when she knew that she was being watched again. She was never really alone. There was always Shar or another trusted charioteer at hand, and no man stepped forth from the thicket shadows.

The years had fled by without her really noticing. Her babies had grown into young women. Cavatina, so lovely with her gay, bright blue eyes, was of a marriageable age. Ceridwen was tall and slim like her father. Her cleverness with the sword and nimble feet made her the pride of the games arena. Her companion was a huge, long-haired grey dog, given to her by Prasutagus, a gift brought back from one of his numerous journeys to Mona, where it seemed that they traded with a large island that was constantly ravaged by the oceans fury. The Celtic Druids who lived there, bred these dogs for hunting wolves.

This animal had been rejected from the pack because of a fault in his hunting prowess. It did not like getting wet and was therefore no use in the hunting field where game frequently ran into a stream to evade capture by washing away their scent.

Prasutagus had noticed its mild manners and gentle mouth and thought that his younger daughter would be safe with it. Once introduced to each other, it became clear that Prasutagus was indeed right. Wherever Ceridwen went so did this wolfhound, so much so that he was called Shadow.

One evening while Shadow was still in his puppy hood when the entire family were in the bath, Ceridwen was shrieking with laughter as they all played in the soapy, warm water. Shadow came looking for his mistress. Possibly he had heard Ceridwen's screams of glee and mistook them for fright and upon seeing his beloved Ceridwen in what he thought was danger, he bounded forwards to save her. Suddenly he realised that his human pup, his adored goddess, was safe with she who made the laws and whose temper had to be respected. Also he noted that he was about to enter that terrible environment of water! A bath! Shadow attempted to come to a standstill on the polished, wet marble floor. His powerful front legs stretched forward in an effort to stop the propelling scuttle, but still the edge of the pool came treacherously closer. In desperation he sat down on his strong haunches.

Growling, and yelps of anguished terror escaped from between his clenched white teeth, which were the size of pigeons' eggs. His ears flapped as if he were about to fly, and his long, grey feathery tail, frantically swished from side to side acting as a brake. He almost skidded to a stop then tilted forwards, wet black nose first. His bulging eyes stared in horror as he slid into the warm, soapy liquid, somersaulting as he did so. The attending servants could not move quickly enough to avoid a thorough soaking

The terrified dog paddled to Ceridwen to seek her approval. Ceridwen in turn looked at her father for guidance, her hand covering her grinning face.

"I like to have my bath with just my human family, Ceridwen. Shadow, if it so pleases him, can take his in the river." Prasutagus's face was alight with merriment. He derived such pleasure from his children's activities.

119

Chapter 29

Ceridwen and her sister found the situation comical and at first giggled and then laughed outright. They decided that even if Shadow got into trouble from their parents, he was a wonderful comedian and had entertained everyone who had not been drenched, and deserved an extra share of food that night. Boudica looked on amused, with a mother's worship of her babies.

Eventually Shadow was lifted out of the bath and docilely led outside by a very angry servant. He shook himself violently to dry his long, silky coat, his ears flip-flopping against his high, noble head, wetting the unfortunate servant even further. She slapped Shadow across his rump with her hand without much aggression for she, like all the other servants, found Shadow a good watchdog. She sent him to his shelter in the stables with his tail between his legs

Prasutagus and Boudica both found Shadow's demonstration of affection for Ceridwen hilarious. It had shown them that in Shadow's care, Ceridwen was as safe as if she were with a guard of the household. The episode with the dog sliding into the bath was a joke for the rest of the evening and despite Ceridwen's fears, he was not punished.

According to Celtic legend, the spear that Prasutagus carried as a staff of office was the Celtic Great Spear of Lugh, which had killed the one-eyed Formorian, Balor. He was king of evil, darkness and winter according to the legend, or Prasutagus had told Boudica when he brought the spear back from Jerusalem, in that remote land at the far end of the Middle Sea. How it had reached there, he could never discover.

The lance had been defiled by dried blood, said to be that of the man who had died on a cross at the bidding of

Tiberius Claudius because he posed a threat to the Roman Empire. Boudica often wondered if he were the young man Prasutagus had spoken of those long years ago when they declared their marriage vows.

Prasutagus had cleansed the spear himself and felt its power. Whoever had forged it had known his art well. The tip was composed of a brightly shining metal like silver, yet was harder than iron, and kept its sheen without rust. The shaft was time-darkened yew wood and it had stood the test of time. Once he had found its centre, it balanced perfectly. As Prasutagus cleansed the shaft, he noticed that the yew wood was inlaid with the same silvery metal as its point. Carved leaves and vines encircled the upper end of the delicate tracery. They looked as if they had actually grown with the tree from which the spear was made. If all the legends held any truth then it was already older than the Great Stone Circle.

"Never," Prasutagus said, "have I seen such a weapon. The merchant who sold it to me haggled only briefly, as if he was in fact in a hurry to dispose of it."

Prasutagus had favoured Ceridwen and allowed her to practise with his favourite weapon. At first the little girl could barely lift the missile, and then her father had shown her the secret of the spear's balance. After that, Ceridwen hefted the great lance above her head and aimed it at the hog's skin, to catch it just behind the ear. Her triumphant smile had radiated to Prasutagus the joy of victory, and his heart had swollen with pride in his youngest daughter.

They seemed to understand each other as if they were old comrades. Prasutagus had once told Boudica that he wondered indeed if Ceridwen was one of his old friends, reborn to aid him now that the years were bowing his back.

"Indeed husband, I too have this sense that Ceridwen, you and I have met in a life before this one more than

121

once." She had felt an affinity with Ceridwen from the moment that she had entered the world.

When Cavatina was sixteen, Prasutagus was concerned about her future and set about searching for a suitable man for her to marry. He called for a feast, and invited as many young princes as he knew, including Caradoc the surviving son of his neighbour, King Cymbeline, now dead these past ten years. Cymbeline's elder son also died in conflict with the Romans.

Either son would have been acceptable as a possible son-by-law or else their male offspring, and would make ideal kings. He also invited wealthy young princes of far away countries, all arriving in time for the celebrations. Most were housed in the Iceni settlement, some as far away as Gariannonum.

Prasutagus decided to invite some of the high-ranking Roman officers and civilians who were contacts of Nero, considering that this would be a diplomatic move to secure the welfare of the Iceni.

Cavatina, when she heard of her father's plans, became very quiet and not the usual exuberant young woman. Eventually Boudica asked her if she were ill. "No, not really. It's just that father has taken it for granted that I wish to marry and I am content to stay here with you and Ceridwen. I know that father is no longer a young man and thinks that he is doing what is best for me before the gods call him to rest, but I would like to live my life here in Icenorum with all my friends. Please do not send me away," she pleaded.

Boudica smiled as she comforted her. "Believe me Cavatina, I do know what you feel, for I too did not wish to leave my family. Yet look how happy we have been. Think also that Ceridwen and you would not have been born if I had stayed at home. For now, we will only look to see what young men there are you might like to get to know better, shall we?" Cavatina agreed with her mother and for the moment the pressure of marriage was eased and Cavatina went about in her usual carefree way.

The feast was a grand success, with ampoules of wine from Gaul. Exotic fruit from all over the known world were imported. Several oxen were roasted over glowing embers in pits dug deep enough to hold a lot of faggots of kindling to last through the night before the banquet, so that next morning the meat was cooked through and tender. Cakes and sweetmeats were made by the servants who had come from different countries, making a mixed selection to suit all tastes.

Harpers played their instruments and sang songs of Cavatina's loveliness just as they had at the wedding of Boudica to Prasutagus, and although Cavatina laughed and danced, she did not allow herself to be singled out by any one young man.

Some, besotted by the beauty of blue-black hair, soft rounded curves and large deep blue eyes, approached Prasutagus with requests for Cavatina's hand in marriage, promising to be able to give her a home equal to that to which she was accustomed. However, Prasutagus knew his daughter well enough not to make promises for her and suggested that first they ask Cavatina!

Occasionally, Boudica noticed her husband lower his chin to rest it on his chest. He would then look at a would-be suitor through half closed eyes. She knew instinctively what he was doing. Prasutagus was peering into the young person's spirit to ascertain his true feelings and see if he was telling the truth. A scowl meant that the would-be suitor was asked to depart. A smile favoured those welcome to stay.

Chapter 30

Most of the Romans invited were inclined to talk among themselves except one man who had mixed parentage - a Roman father and a mother from Gaul. After a leading Roman merchant had introduced him officially as Julius Classicus to Prasutagus and Boudica, he walked about talking to the local people. He paid careful attention to Cavatina and Ceridwen, listening to the young girls chatter, his eyes never straying from their faces. From time to time his gaze fastened on Boudica, and his face became quizzical, as if he was asking himself a question.

Then he strolled back to his hosts, goblet in hand, his eyes peering over the rim. Silently he toasted Boudica! The colour rose in her cheeks. She felt that she knew this man. It was he who had appeared as if by magic by the waterfall. What was he doing there? Who was he really watching, and why?

Prasutagus's eyes opened wide, then half closed. He peered at Julius Classicus, and then made a sound as if clearing his throat. He turned to his wife and led her away to where Leofric and several other Druids sat discussing the finer points of the theory that there was one master hand in control and production of the earth.

"... I firmly maintain that we live one life so that we can learn what we must do in the next. Whoever controls this way of bringing us to enlightenment must surely be great indeed! ..." An elderly lady whose eyes were dim and back bent with time was giving her opinion.

Prasutagus waited respectfully for her to complete what she wanted to say, before he introduced her to Boudica as Gildelma. The old crone held Boudica's hand then her toothless mouth split into a grin.

"Ah, my queen, I've been waiting for you. We are to be companions in our search for truth. There is so much to learn and so little time in which to do it. I will teach you as much wisdom as you are capable of absorbing." Gildelma was now chuckling. "And you my lovely lady, you will carry this knowledge with you throughout all eternity!"

"Come, old mother, let us not get too involved with such serious matters as eternity at my daughters' party. It is a time for merriment," Prasutagus said and gave Gildelma a plate of sweetmeats to pick from.

Gildelma glanced up at the king with watchful eyes. "Yes my lord, let us be happy whilst we can!" and took a mouthful of mead as her hand reached out for the tasty morsels offered to her.

After spending time with his Druid companions, Prasutagus led Boudica back to their guests and the festivities.

Boudica noticed that her husband seemed preoccupied, but he continued as a genial host making all welcome. Then Boudica saw his eyes alight on a newcomer who had obviously ridden a long way in a hurry. The young man's face was moist with perspiration and his horse lathered.

He gave the reins of his exhausted horse to a waiting groom, and then brushed down his clothes, which were of the Roman fashion of white kilt and toga. He advanced into the feasting area where Boudica and Prasutagus held court for their guests.

He came smiling and held a gift out for Cavatina, a bejewelled bracelet, and bowed to Prasutagus, then Boudica. "My Lord, my Lady," he said, still smiling, "Your invitation failed to reach me in time to be here at the acceptable moment. Please forgive me." He went to bend forward to kiss Boudica's fingertips, but Prasutagus moved ahead of him and stood in his path.

"I have no recollection off having issued an invitation to you, sir," Prasutagus said with an ice edge to his normally soft voice.

The visitor flushed slightly at the veiled insult. His features reminded Boudica of an emissary of the gods. His face was lightly tanned by warm suns. He had jet-black hair with a stray lock that hung over his incredibly blue eyes which had a green centre, giving him a look of a lost child yet he had an air of debauchery.

"My name is Marius Sextus, my father is..."

"Yes, I know who your parents are, and as I am King of Icenorum Venta, my daughter Cavatina will one day reign in my place. The young men invited here to-day are those I consider suitable to be her consort." Prasutagus left no room for doubt as to what he thought of Marius.

Marius glanced up at Boudica. Standing tall, she was now thirty-four years of age. Her hair was as it had been when she had landed for the first time in Britain to be Prasutagus's bride. It was a mass of silk soft, red-gold curls. The yielding downy cushions of her breasts, and rounded plump thighs made her an even finer-looking woman than she had as a virgin of eighteen years.

Marius grunted with embarrassment as his cheeks flushed with desire. "Your pardon, my Lord, my Lady," he said as he backed away and held his toga across his body to shield the symbol of his craving lust.

The feast ended with a disappointed group of young men. Cavatina had chosen none of them, and secretly Prasutagus was pleased. He had no real wish for his daughter to leave. It was his hope that she would one day be safe and well cared for when he was taken to the gods. He seemed to see her still as a little girl needing his care instead of a woman in her late youth and ripe for a lover's embrace.

Later in the year as the autumn leaves started to fall, Boudica was surprised to find Shar loading Prasutagus's large travelling chariot with the necessities for a long journey. Before she could ask him where he was going, Prasutagus came and joined them.

"Wife! You are about early this day. I was coming to tell you that it is time for me to go to Mona and declare

Cavatina and Ceridwen my legal heirs." He looked down at his feet, obviously embarrassed that he had neglected to speak to Boudica sooner. She realised that her dear husband was aged, weary of life, and his memory was no longer to be relied upon.

"Yes, my lord, I agree with you. You travel without me?" she asked.

Prasutagus lifted his grey head, his drained smile telling Boudica more than words that he needed to be alone for this particular voyage. Then as she studied his face, it dawned on her that Prasutagus was going much further than Mona. "You journey beyond Mona, my lord, for a reason that you cannot tell me?" It was a statement that became a question.

"Ha, wife, I can keep no secret from you now that you have studied the ways of the Druid." His look was now more intense. He's to tell me that he will not return, she thought, and her heart somersaulted in her breast.

"When Morrigu, the Queen of the Dead calls for me, I would like to think that I have protected you and our children from the evils of this world. Therefore do not be distressed when I name the Roman, Lord Nero and our two daughters as my heirs. I do so for a very good reason, my beloved." Prasutagus sat down to rest upon a shady bench then continued to tell Boudica what she needed to know before he left. Also, he wanted her to hear it from him and not from the Druid notary.

Chapter 31

"You are so beautiful and full of passionate life, I could not bear it if I thought that by leaving you Icenorum, I would be condemning you to the attentions of every gold seeking, money hungry young man in all of the Roman empire. No, my love! You are well provided for. Our children adore you and will never see you want for anything, and Nero is a good ruler. His shrewdness will be of use to our lands."

Prasutagus placed his arm about Boudica's shoulders. "My love for you wife, does not blind me to the fact that you are still young and excitingly vigorous. Men will admire you for many years to come, and if one arrives who loves you for yourself and not the Iceni lands and gold, then marry him after Morrigu takes me." There was a sad certainty in Prasutagus's words and Boudica found that she could not argue with his wisdom.

"My journey will take me far, far away my beloved. I have been commissioned by our Chief Druid Leofric, to go to a land of mighty mountains beyond the middle sea, to seek out the holy monks who live in isolation there. It is said of them that they have proof of the gift of eternal life and look for their dead ruler in the shape of a newborn baby. These monks are so enlightened that I long to be with them and share their understanding." Prasutagus breathed deeply. His face had taken on a waxy hue and there was dew on his forehead.

"Must you go?" Boudica asked of him. "Cannot a younger man go instead?"

"A younger man is coming with me to share this new information. Junus has completed his training and is thirsty for knowledge of the countries that we shall visit. He will carry all the newly acquired knowledge back with him, once we have learned everything we can." Boudica noticed that her husband did not include himself in the return journey.

She knew that this was Prasutagus's last trip into the unknown world. His wanderlust was driving him to spend his last days on earth away from those he loved most.

They embraced, and then Shar mounted his horse, carrying the long spear of Prasutagus's authority. Prasutagus, now nearly eighty years old, stepped up into his waiting chariot where a charioteer held the reins. He looked down at Boudica. Their daughters had joined her out of curiosity to see what their father was doing,

Boudica could see that Prasutagus' heart was heavy and tried to smile encouragement to him, just as her brother Sven had tried to give her moral support when she was to meet Prasutagus for the first time.

As he was about to leave, Prasutagus turned in his chariot. There was a wry smile on his face. "Boudica, I have no fear of leaving our children's welfare in your capable hands and Shadow's guardianship, for I have witnessed the displeasure that you displayed when you considered them in any trouble. Also I have seen you nurse them when they suffered their baby troubles of cutting teeth. Even as I stand here I see the beautiful blue aura of truth that floats around you." Prasutagus smiled as he thought of the treatment of any man who would attempt to delude Boudica where her daughters were concerned. He would meet with a raging wild she wolf.

"Any man who comes calling for the hands of either of our daughters needs to be well endowed with both good parentage and wealthy lands!" Prasutagus's eyes twinkled. Obviously he cherished deeply the two daughters she had given him, Cavatina and Ceridwen.

" I have watched you while you slept and seen the wonderful golden light of love manifest itself around you, my dearest. My home is safe in your hands, my dear wife, and I'll make you safe in mine."

He leaned forward towards Boudica and then he passed his left hand across her face, obscuring her eyes momentarily. "Wake up my child. You are free." Then he whispered so that only she could hear, "Also remember the gold in the cave!"

"Ceridwen, my child, come here!" he commanded his younger daughter. Prasutagus retrieved his spear from Shah and held it above his head. "Take this, for you are able to use it well enough now. Carry it with you always for it has magical powers to protect its owner."

"Father, you must take it with you. It is your talisman and brings you good luck. It will bring you safely home again to us!" she pleaded.

"No. The gods have decreed that you are to be the next to carry this emblem. A mighty god came to me in my sleep. He told me that you are the rightful owner of this weapon. I was the guardian until you were of age to carry it, therefore you must obey me and the gods!" Prasutagus's face was now as fierce as his family had ever seen it. The calm, soft grey eyes were stormy and his gentle mouth a harsh thin line, so that Ceridwen quivered at his overbearing attitude and took the proffered lance.

Then Prasutagus nodded his head at Shar to let him know that he was now ready to leave. The charioteer flipped the horses' reins and bid them move out. A cavalcade of soldiers escorted him from the settlement as he made his way to the Roman road to Ratae Corianorum, then on to Mona.

As his chariot disappeared, Boudica felt as if she had been immersed in a pool of ice-cold water. She heaved a deep breath and looked about to see if anyone had noticed. Prasutagus had said something almost in a whisper about being free. He had called her a child!

Taking her daughters by their hands she went into the villa that had been her home for over nineteen years and looked around as though seeing it for the first time. It was as if she had spent those years in a dream and had as Prasutagus said, woken up.

The sounds of life within the settlement continued. Women sang as they went about caring for their homes, the blacksmith's hammer still ping-tanged on the anvil in his smithy and children still played and laughed in the square.

Boudica felt as though she was listening to the sounds for the first time. Her memory took her back to the day when she first came to the lands of the Iceni to be the bride of their king, Prasutagus.

Chapter 32

He had helped her to step from the longboat to the land and they had exchanged glances. He had escorted her to... No! Go back. They had shared each other's glances, and then he had looked so deeply into her eyes that she felt as though her very soul had been laid bare. Realisation came as a shock. Prasutagus had cast his spell upon her. She was his bond slave from that day onwards until to day when he had set her free.

She had looked upon Prasutagus as if he was a handsome lover and she had come to love him dearly. How foolish was my lord Prasutagus, she reflected. He was so kind to my babies and me. How could I not love him?

Boudica took her girls by the hand and led them back into the beautiful home that her husband had given them. She prepared for the day's work of giving judgement to the small problems of the community.

Prasutagus went from his home to Mona in the far west of Britain, where he made his will and left a copy in the hands of the High priests. He journeyed with a Junus, a newly fledged Druid, to the lands of the Middle Sea where his wanderlust had taken him. Boudica had no more news of him though he continued to send home gifts for his family and friends.

One day Boudica had felt an overwhelming sense of loss. It was as if a cold wind of winter had blown over her, leaving her shivering in the afternoon sunshine. This was long before the message of his death reached her.

She knew in her heart that Prasutagus had left her to sleep forever, and the grief that she felt was if her life no longer had any meaning. It made her so morose that her daughters feared for her health. She went about her duties of dispensing justice and overseeing changes or alterations within the community as if in a dream, and she continued to serve everyone to the best of her ability, earning the respect of all.

Then Leofric, the Druid chieftain who brought the sad news, was aware that this message was not unexpected and that Boudica was already in mourning for her husband for there was a look of a lost soul about her, even though she fully believed in eternal life and knew that they would be reunited eventually.

Leofric told her of the rites of passage that were to be given for Prasutagus at the Stone circle. It would start to take place as the moon was at its fullest and would continue until the moon was but a slim sliver of light in the night sky. It would light Prasutagus' journey to the next world and his spirit would be appeased even though his body was resting in that far off land.

Later in the year, Marius, the prince of northern descent, whom Prasutagus had turned away at the feast, came to visit Icenorum again on the pretext of asking for the hand of Cavatina in marriage. Really he wanted to determine which of the women would be the best one to court. He had made the justifiable mistake in thinking that Boudica would be Prasutagus' natural heir and therefore the wealthiest.

Boudica spotted his ploy as soon as his eyes cast around for the evidence of riches. They alighted on the rich tapestry hangings in the villa and the pure-bred horses in the stables. So, a pretty boy comes to pay his respects to my daughter, yet his thoughts are on our wealth, she surmised.

Playing him at his own game she invited him to stay for a few days and had a banquet served for him. The next day Boudica organised a hunting party to which Marius was again invited. Ceridwen shared a chariot with her mother, but Cavatina decided that she did not like to see wild animals slaughtered and stayed at home.

The hunt went well. Several wild boar were potted, some of which were plump young suckling pigs like the one that Shar had caught and cooked for them. Boudica was reminded of the journey from the Stone Circle on her wedding day with Prasutagus.

The hunting party was now ready to return home and Boudica's thoughts were with her husband whose last words to her had been about taking a lover, but being careful to whom she got betrothed.

Marius had shared the chariot with her and Ceridwen, and he was about to throw his spear at a hare that was leaping about in a hay field when Boudica stopped him.

"The hare is troubled. There is menace brewing. Can't you see that he is trying to tell us something, Marius?" she asked. Her voice was harsh at such a stupid action as taking the life of an oracle. "See, he is now leaping and twisting in mid-air. I warn you Marius, danger is on its way!"

Marius laid his spear down again frowning. He seemed to resent being corrected in front of Ceridwen, more like a spoilt child than a suitor and possible husband for Cavatina, thought Boudica.

The sound of marching feet brought the party to a standstill whilst a contingent of the Roman army crossed their path on the newly made road. The officer at the head of the marching column was riding a tall grey stallion. He lifted his head and glanced at her, then raised a hand in salute. There was a merry knowing glow in his eyes.

He was wearing his full uniform of boiled leather body armour, high-laced sandals, and deep blue cloak and kilt. His head was bare. He carried a white and gold staff of office in his fist. His standard bearer carried a pennant with the image of a mythical creature, half goat and half fish, called a Capricorn.

At first Boudica did not recognise him. Then she noticed his dark, curling hair, and deep bronzed features. His eyes she saw, were a soft liquid brown, his lips were full, and his torso powerful. She knew who he was! Julius Classicus, her lover from the waterfall in the woods and at Cavatina's party. Was he was still watching over her?

Chapter 33

The hunting party waited until all the soldiers had gone by then continued with the chase. Boudica was excited at the sight of her lover, but she kept her secret even though she was now a widow and could take a lover with impunity.

As the sun was about to descend, the hunting party made their way back to Icenorum. A wolf blocked the path. Boudica called a halt and looked carefully at the animal. It was a she wolf with empty paps that hung down slackly from her ribs. The bitch had young and had been unable to catch food for her pups and her and for many days, Boudica was certain, she had been starving.

Alighting from her chariot she went to the supply cart and picked out the plump young hog. Without a care for her safety, she took it to the waiting wolf. She spoke in low tones to the animal so that the rest of the party could hear. The wolf lowered her head as if to give obeisance to a queen, then picked up the offering in her great jaws and made off into the woods and her lair.

Marius was astounded! It would have been perilous for a fully armed man to approach a starving wolf, yet this woman had taken it a gift of food and the animal had bowed to her. Like Prasutagus before him, he wondered what kind of mortal this woman was.

"Why did you do that?" he demanded.

"Marius, my wolf-skin cape is starting to moult. I need a new one and where do you think wolf- skin capes come from?" Boudica resented Marius's outburst. He was about to learn that the Iceni Queen could have a sharp tongue when it suited her.

"When the wolf cubs are the right size and the snow is about to fall, you can collect pelts for me, bearing in mind that a healthy young male is not so easily killed as a half starved bitch." The veiled slight to his valour and prowess bit deeply.

Marius remained silent for the rest of the journey while Ceridwen chatted happily about the wolf and how much like Shadow it was. "I wonder if we could catch a pup and give it to Shadow as a friend?" she asked her mother blithely.

"I do not think that Shadow would see a wolf pup as a companion, Ceridwen," Boudica replied, laughing. How like her daughter to see friendship in the most doubtful places.

The feast that night on wild boar was joined by most of the villagers who brought with them contributions in the form of freshly grown crops, most of which had been introduced by the invading Romans, who had needed them to feed the troops.

Julius Classicus arrived as the festivities began to wind down for the night. As his gaze settled on Marius, his expression hardened. Boudica wondered if there was bad blood between them. Did Julius know of her clandestine association with Marius? Indeed, did either one know anything of the other?

To remove any chance of ill feeling between them, she produced some of the wine that Prasutagus had brought back from the Roman capital some years before he left for his last journey.

Strange, she thought, you seem to be in my thoughts a lot today, my husband. Is it because of the young prince Marius or the Roman officer? Her mind was far away as she hugged the ampoule of wine to her bosom, not daring to trust it to a servant. Taking care not to drop the precious liquid, she made her way to the festivities.

Julius made his excuses and left at daybreak, while Marius stayed for two more days' hunting and chariot racing. Then he bade Boudica and her two daughters farewell, promising to return as soon as he had been to Gariannonum to visit relatives.

Boudica took a long, hard look at her departing guest and knew that he was not suitable for a son by law! You like the good things in life but you are not prepared to pay the proper price for them. I'll have some fun with you and let Cavatina learn of your perfidy.

The morning star shone brightly as Marius left the front courtyard. Rush lights lit the gentle pearly dawn, sending shadows of deep purple where the light of the flickering flames did not reach.

Boudica watched Marius leave. Like a ghost, he made his way to the outer courtyard where he had left his chariot and as he passed one particularly badly lit place, the bushes stirred and Julius Classicus's grey horse stepped daintily from the shelter of the thicket and blocked his way.

The next thing that she witnessed astounded her. Julius dismounted and she heard him say, "My horse seems to be lame, Marius. Would you mind holding its bridle for me whilst I examine its hoofs?" Julius's face was bland, almost friendly as he dismounted and held the reins to Marius.

As he bent over the hoof of his horse, Julius Classicus silently and cunningly withdrew the sharp knife that he kept strapped to his waist, swung around and plunged it into Marius's back. The blade slid into his soft flesh like a lover going to his mistress.

Boudica could not believe her eyes. Why? Why had Julius murdered Marius? It could not be out of jealousy for her favours, surely? No, that could not possibly be the answer.

She was transfixed as Julius placed Marius's body in his chariot then mounting his grey, he led the harnessed horses away. Without a backward glance he took with him all evidence of his evil act.

Julius appeared to show no sign of remorse. In fact there seemed to be a glint of malice reflected from the rush lights in his eyes.

Boudica felt a shiver of dread, colder than the winds from the north in the depths of winter. She wondered if Julius had noticed her and if he had, did he care that she knew him to be a murderer? Hurriedly, she pulled her cloak about her shoulders. With her head held down, she went back into her villa in deep reflection, for as much as she adored Julius, she abhorred murder. It went against all that she believed in. Even Thor, the god of her homeland would not consent to the death of an innocent man. Warriors expected death and welcomed it in battle. To die with a battle-axe in his hand, a warrior was certain to enter Valhalla. But to be murdered?

Chapter 34

As a high-ranking Roman officer, Julius Classicus formed part of the escort taking Boudica to the Rites of Passage for Prasutagus. He replaced Suetonius Paulinus, the Roman general in control of Britain, who was attending to work on the roads leading to Caledonia.

Julius attended to the entire organisation of the event for such a nobleman as the King of the Iceni, marshalling Roman soldiers as well as the Iceni aristocracy who were to attend.

Boudica had little to say to Julius on the journey south, keeping to her own chariot with her daughters for company. They would be initiated into the roll of joint queens at the next new moon.

The shock of seeing Julius perform such an atrocity had upset her deeply and the question as to why, remained unanswered.

As the widow Boudica stood beside the High Druid Leofric as he chanted the prayers for Prasutagus, pleading with Morrigu to lead him to safety and let his next life be full of happiness.

Food had been prepared for the travellers and songs were sung but not the joyful melodies of the wedding. These were telling all who would listen about Prasutagus's deeds, including the one about the giant fish that he slew. They told of his travels and the knowledge that he had brought back from distant lands, and his ability to cure people with wild herbs. Nothing was told of his abilities to cast spells; yet Boudica was conscious that the harpers must have known. They had seen his work and watched him for years.

On the return journey, Boudica dismissed her escort, sending her daughters with them and led Julius to where Prasutagus and she had shared their first night together as husband and wife. She needed to know why Classicus had slain Marius, something she could not question him about in public.

The gloom in the small valley of ancient trees helped by casting concealing shadows across Classicus's face. Boudica asked very softly, "Why did you end the life of Marius?"

Julius spun around to face her, and then lowered his head to mask his thoughts. "He was a danger to Rome. He had been carrying messages to the wild people of the far north telling of movements of the Roman army. I had orders from Suetonius to execute him." Julius mopped his brow with a piece of fine cloth and still did not look directly at his companion.

Boudica felt that she had been given a half-truth. The complete reason for the death of Marius would remain a secret known only to Julius.

"Come my lady, do not bother your head with the young fool. The night is cool and my arms ache for you."

Boudica could not refuse the throbbing pain in her loins for Julius even though the grove of oak trees whispered a warning to her as she lay beside him.

The murdered Marius was a prince of the royal blood of Caledonia. Why would he betray his country with information as to when and where to attack? Boudica had not seen Julius Classicus since the hunt when he had killed Marius. Now she needed the warmth of a virile man's body close to her. Also the demands made by her flesh were overpowering and she ignored the forest's caution with the compulsion to feel alive. She disregarded Prasutagus's warning and that of the ever-sagacious oak trees in her desire for fulfilment as a woman.

With the hunger of her body appeased, Boudica hastened home alone. Julius had ridden west to oversee some road construction.

Boudica decided that for the present, she would need to keep her own council and say nothing about the assassination of Marius, not even to Garian the head man of the Iceni settlement.

On her arrival, she was confronted by the sight of huge Roman wagons loaded with grain and sheep carcases pulling away from the stores and slaughterhouses.

She pulled her chariot in front of the departing farm carts to stop them from leaving. "What means this?" she demanded of the lead waggoner.

"It means my lady that you are paying your share of the costs of keeping the peace in this land of Iceni," the man replied.

"On whose orders?"

"On the express orders of the legate at Camulodunum. Take it up with him if you have any complaints, though I should warn you, he has been instructed to do so by our lord Nero."

Boudica stood stock-still. Nero was supposed to be a fine leader and what was more he was party to Prasutagus's will. How could this be, she wondered?

"Believe me, madam, I act under orders as does every other man serving the Lord Nero!" He prepared to take his team and wagon out onto the road. "My Lord Nero is a changed man, Lady. It seems that the more he has the more he wants, and I for one do not intend to disobey his commands." He chucked to the horses, pulling on the leads to direct them to the road. His look and words told her that he would return for more supplies very soon.

Trembling and white with anger, she returned to her villa to make certain that it had not been raided. Nothing had been taken yet, though she knew that it would not be long before the plundering thieves would be back for the gold and jewels amassed by Prasutagus.

That night she made up her mind to hide as much of the wealth as she could in the flint cave and wondered whom she could trust. There was only one man of any worth who sprang to her mind, and he was old and wise Garian who had welcomed Ceridwen into the world.

Wrapping a dark cloak about her shoulders to lessen the chance of being noticed in the brilliant moonlight, Boudica stole from the villa by a back door, and made her way to Garian's home.

She tapped lightly, and the door was opened almost immediately. Garian stood before her. He seemed to know why she was visiting so late at night.

My Lady, welcome. Come in if it pleases you."

"Garian, the thieving Romans are plundering our winter stores. We will be without food to last us through the hungry months."

Garian agreed with her saying, "Yes, my Lady, and the only way that we are going to survive is to hide our precious food before they return for more."

"Where can we be certain of hiding our provisions without them being discovered?"

"The Fens are treacherous to those who do not know them and there are places where only an Iceni dare go, my Lady. I will start moving grain and goods tonight. Now, do not be anxious. Return to the villa. I will come and see you when the work is done."

"Garian, there is also the question of the Iceni wealth, the gold and jewels that Prasutagus gathered on his numerous voyages to those distant lands. I cannot allow them to fall into the hands of that tyrant Nero. Oh, how my Lord Prasutagus was deceived by him."

Garian lowered his head. His love for his King was well known and his attitude displayed his bitter disappointment by this flaw in Prasutagus.

"My Queen, even a well-informed man like our King, a Druid Priest, can make mistakes, though with his spiritual abilities being able to see into a man's soul, it is a surprise!" Garian shook his head. The years of being the settlement's headman had taught him to take a closer view of every problem from different angles.

"King Prasutagus was, to my mind, much worn by his years and it could be that he did not consider the

143

possibility of a man in Nero's position, to change. The fact that he was Roman with a family history of assassinations, should have given him some warning though."

Garian's voice was sad. There had been too much change of late, and he was not much younger than Prasutagus had been when he died.

" He had a very good hiding place for your valuables in the flint mines. Did you know this?" he asked.

"Yes, but there are also those items of gold and jewels that we use every day. These too must be hidden. I'll get them ready packed in a stout leather pouch and if you'll collect them as the sun rises tomorrow, they can go at first light."

Garian bowed his head and led Boudica to the door. "Now my Queen, I go to find the people to help move the stores. I bid you goodnight," he said as he ushered her out into the night, and like a phantom, she departed into the dank mist to go to her home.

Chapter 35

Once inside the villa, Boudica went about collecting any item that would be of value to the Roman invaders. As the sun god came up over the Germanic Sea, she had loaded a working chariot with those possessions of worth.

Garian came towards her out of the foggy dawn. He was ready for a long journey. "Good day, my Lady," he said, and then noticed that she was still in the robes that she had worn when visiting him the night before. "My Lady, you must be weary. Go and sleep I beg you, for you are needed to be strong for the coming battles."

"There will be no wars Garian. This is just a precaution against our Roman friends being avaricious for the Iceni wealth."

"I feel that blood will be spilt because the Romans know of the wealth of Prasutagus and will surely come looking for it. They will have no mercy and we will need to fight for our very lives, Madam. I scent it in the air."

Memories of Betulanter, the old woman at Dere Well, and her prophesy, came to her mind. Without thinking, Boudica's reply to her good friend was brusque, "Then the sooner this load is hidden, the better. Get to your horse and let us be out of here before the sun god goes to sleep."

Keeping to the old pedlars' route and out of sight of the Roman cavalry, they headed to the old flint mines. After several grinding days, they arrived, bone weary. Boudica remembered the fight that Prasutagus had with the pike fish and spoke to Uriticor about it.

"Ahh, that was a wonderful sight. Never have I seen such a monster and to think our king killed it with his spear. We sing songs of it still and remember you, my Lady, when you poked it in the eye to escape from it. It could have been any one of my people here who met up with it and they would have died." Uriticor heaved a huge sigh as he recollected the experience. He led them to the mineshaft and assisted Boudica and Garian to descend into the pit.

With nearly all of the Iceni wealth now hidden safely, Boudica felt confident that her home would be safe from the marauding Roman army.

She asked for a woman servant to help her to bathe in the pool, and a small dwelling was given to her for her to rest in afterwards.

The evening water was cool and refreshing as she swam to the centre of the lake. Brown trout with their black spots and square tail fins, idled past, roach with their bright red eyes glared, chub with lines along their sides and dark scales like a network and little sticklebacks, darted everywhere. The pool was alive with fish again. Boudica dived to where she had met the gigantic pike. Nothing stirred the underwater weeds except the usual harmless fish. Her swim, uninterrupted by malevolent pike was lazy and relaxed. She rocketed to the surface, swam on her back and then dived again, to enjoy the soft movements of water about her tired limbs.

On her return to the surface, she noticed a shadow on the dark water. Perhaps it's my dressing maid, she thought, but as she waded ashore, there was no woman standing with a drying cloth, only her lover from the woods, Julius Classicus.

He held the cloth out to her and helped her to wrap it around her damp body. His features were hardly discernible in the deepening twilight. He said nothing as he placed the wolf-skin cloak about her. Her heart was hammering in her breast. What did he want? Why was he here?

His breath on her cheek answered these questions and posed more. Where could they go where they would not be disturbed? Her lover had these problems solved as he led her to where he had a small racing chariot with two slender horses in the harness.

The swift, high stepping geldings were heading due east. They galloped as if their lives depended on it. Then with her lover's aid, Boudica stepped down when they reached a deserted crossroads in a clearing. A small flint and thatch building stood to one side, to which she was led, then as he closed the door to a circular room he spoke to her. "My lady, take care. I know that you hide your wealth and I will never betray you, but there are others who might, for the price of their heads. Trust no one, I beg of you." His plea came as a shock to Boudica. How much more did he know and how?

"One day I hope to be able to claim you as mine and you will have no need for the Iceni gold. My family is not without such things."

While he had been talking, he had removed the cloak and was holding her close, the heat from his body warming her, his lips exploring her neck and ears. She could feel his trunk-like legs hard against her thighs. Then as he kissed her mouth, he lowered her gently to the rush-strewn floor.

Later Boudica asked of him, "Julius, what is it that you want of me? You have a family and a place at Nero's side, yet you haunt me!"

"My lady, I cannot live without you. I trust that one day you will take me as your consort," he replied.

"What difference would that make to you, Julius?"

"I would be acting king of the Iceni and help you govern your lands."

"Julius, do you not know that I am a pauper, that my daughters and your noble Nero are the inheritors of the Iceni domain?"

There was a searching look upon her face that Julius found disconcerting. His startled expression was enough to tell her that perhaps Prasutagus had been wise to cut her out of his will so that any would-be suitor would indeed marry her for herself and not her wealth.

147

She laughed gaily with relief at her escape from the entanglement of marriage with the kind of man that Julius was. He would no doubt smart under the ignominy of being found out as a fortune hunter, but his love of the luxury of the villa at Icenorum would drag him back, she surmised.

The return journey to the flint mines was made without either of them speaking and he took her back to the edge of the pool in a place of deep shadow.

He held her hand for a moment and kissed her fingertips before he disappeared silently with his chariot into the night.

Her dressing maid had fallen asleep, wrapped up in a thick cloak of flax and wool. She would take no harm from the night chill Boudica decided; therefore she did not disturb her slumbers.

Next morning with Garian, she returned to Icenorum Venta as if she had been out on a night's hunting, nothing more, and continued to live a normal life of hunting and chariot racing.

As Boudica lay on her couch that night, she thought deeply about Julius's proposal. He wanted, not just her, but also all of the Iceni lands and wealth. He considered himself fit to wear the helmet of Prasutagus. This must never be, she decided. Silently, so as not to disturb her waiting maids, she made her way to the room where Prasutagus had kept his herbs and made his potions. A picture of the contents of every herb was drawn on the storage phials. She took one with the tansy herb on it that she knew well and another that had been imported by the Romans that they called rue. This was for those women who had loved unwisely such as she. The mixing and infusing to make the medicine were soon accomplished. It tasted even more bitter than Julius's assumption that he could rule her and the Iceni. But this remedy would ensure that at no time would he have a hold over her. She would take this and drink it as if it were nectar for as much as her being ached for his love and caresses, no child of Julius Classicus could replace the children of her lord and king, Prasutagus.

One day much later in the year, she invited him to the Sacred Circle to winter celebrations, to greet the return of the sun god. After which they had gone to the secret hideout on the return drive. Snow had fallen and they had left their careless tracks for any one passing to see. As they huddled beneath the wolfskin cloak, their hungry passion was soon spent.

Suddenly Boudica felt the need to return to Icenorum Venta and her children. Her mother's instinct was telling her that all was not well with Ceridwen and Cavatina. Hurriedly she thrust aside the fur, stood up adjusting her long skirt and bent down to retrieve her cloak before fastening it about her shoulders. "My children need me. I must hurry, I'll see you at the meeting house in Camulodunum when you journey back to Gariannonum." She spoke quickly, in her haste to be away.

Chapter 36

She mounted her chariot to gallop away at breakneck speed eastwards. Wasting no time for respite, she arrived home in time to be confronted by Ceridwen tending Cavatina, who was sobbing with grief.

Leaping down from her chariot, Boudica could see that her children had suffered a brutal assault. The gold torques that Prasutagus had given them on their twelfth birthdays were missing, blood ran down the girls' legs and their shifts were torn to shreds.

Her babies had been violated!

Rage, like she had never felt before, tore through Boudica. Her heart beat a staccato, thudding fit to burst from the confines of her ribs. A red haze dulled her sight as she looked around for the culprit.

Whoever had done this deed must pay. "Ceridwen, who did this to you, my child?" she asked as tenderly as her wrath would allow. The young girl looked up at her mother and saw the fury in her eyes. "Mother, it was not a man of the Iceni," she assured her mother. "Cavatina and I were playing in the brook that runs to the sea. We had our dogs and our maids with us, but these big men wore soldiers uniforms, like Romans and they killed the dogs and hurt the maids the same as they did us."

Ceridwen's tears swamped Boudica's shift as she held her head to her mother's breast. Stroking her child's fair hair, she caressed her gently, whispering soothing words that only a parent can. Then she called to the waiting maids and gave instructions for the warm bathing pool to be made ready. The girls were to be bathed and put to rest in their rooms, with a maid to stay in attendance on them.

The next morning a trusted maid was called to take Cavatina to Dere Well and take the neck cloth as proof of identity to Fililpenda, and ask her to care for Cavatina who had suffered so much shock as to be out of her mind.

Boudica knew that her child would be in the best of hands with the bereaved mother.

With her sick daughter safely in Dere Well, Boudica was now going to find out who was responsible for children's assault!

Her horses were tired from the gallop home the previous night so she had a pair of young strong stallions harnessed in their place. These animals had been fed oats as well as straw to give them the stamina to pull the heavy working chariots and were pulling at their bits, anxious to be away.

The light chariot flew down the Roman road towards Camulodunum. Briefly Boudica thought to call at Gariannonum to enquire about Julius's return, but she dismissed it. It would only take up precious time. She would however call on the King of Camulodunum and leader of the Trivantes. His knowledge of the Roman garrison would be of assistance though Boudica had heard that he and his family were at war among themselves. Also the Romans treated the people of Trivantes no better than slaves.

Perhaps Caradoc could tell her whom to approach about such malicious behaviour by Roman soldiers. She must find those responsible or die in the attempt.

The desolation that she felt at her children's grievous treatment ate away at her spirit. She knew that she could never rest all the time she did not have retribution, Andraste the earth goddess willing, no girl was ever deflowered without her consent, and no man had the right to hurt a child in any manner, whatsoever! She would have her revenge on these sadistic, Roman beasts. They called themselves enlightened and would teach the Iceni their laws and ways. Her anger sent these thought around her head, making it spin.

Boudica held the reins to the horses loosely and gave them their head as they galloped on towards the North gate of Camulodunum.

The long, tiring journey had made the horses lather and Boudica led them into Caradoc's stables. As a groom came out to tend them, Caradoc himself came to welcome her to his home, a villa built similarly to Prasutagus's home.

"What brings you here all in a lather, madam?" he asked, noting her high colour.

"My daughters have been violated by those Roman soldiers who call themselves civilised!" she spat out as she alighted.

"How can I be of assistance to you, my lady?" He knew all about the rape of young girls by the conquering army, among his own people.

"Take me to their commander. I would have words with him!"

"My Lady Queen, be advised, the Romans think nothing a child's innocence, believe me, for I have witnessed this many times."

"And you did nothing?"

"Yes, I too complained and when I returned home, found my brother dead, and my wife and children had been treated as animals."

"What further harm can they do to me?"

"My Lady, heed my warning and take care. These Romans are worse than any other pillaging army. They will make you pay in a manner that we can not even imagine."

Still Boudica insisted that she be directed to the garrison head quarters to confront its commander.

After she had stated her case against the soldiers who had raped her children, the commander merely smirked and called his aides.

"This woman's carping voice is annoying me. Take her out to the market place and give her back a few lashes. Let others see what happens to troublesome people." He sat down at his desk thinking that that was the last that he would hear from her!

With her hands shackled to the whipping post in the square, Boudica's shift was torn to the waist to bare her flesh to the scourge, and was thrashed as a common criminal.

If she had been annoyed before her meeting with the station commander, now she was seething. How dare these immoral soldiers rape her babies, then horse whip her, the Queen of the Iceni, she fumed to herself.

Friendly Trinovatians undid the shackles and took care of her wounds. Caradoc came to enquire after her well-being. "Please Lady, go back to your children and take care of them for there is nothing that you can do to put matters right."

"No! I cannot put matters right, as you say, but I can stop them from doing any further harm to my children and the children of my people. If you and your people are with me, we will oust these slaughterers of innocents and send them back to their Lord Nero!"

Caradoc gasped with amazement. Go against Rome? The very thought sent tremors of fear down his spine.

"Of course if you do not have the courage of a woman then I must needs wage this war on my own!"

"My lady, I did not say that I would not join you. This is a bold thing that you plan. It will take a brave and well-armed army to defeat them. Do the Iceni have the arms and do they have your courage?"

"You question the loyalty of the Iceni, or their bravery? My people are near to starving because of the Romans. My daughters are not the only young Iceni girls to be ravaged; I can assure you that we will rise up against these oppressors and win."

Caradoc saw the hard, set line of Boudica's mouth, the grim cast to her eyes and knew she spoke truly.

On her return to Icenorum Venta, Boudica called Garian to her villa and told him what had occurred in Camulodunum. She told him that Caradoc and his people, would be joining the Iceni against the Romans.

Chapter 37

"We will need plenty of arrows and some strong bows for our men to fight with. Some of the gold hidden in the flint mines can be used to pay for them. We will also buy as much grain as we can from our neighbours; we need to be well fed before we start our campaign."

"My lady Queen, the Romans are strong and well organised. They are also heavily armed. Is this a wise move?"

"No, Garian not wise, but to allow these barbarians to ride over our necks as if we were less than human, is wrong. They must be shown that the gods venerate life, and a virgin's blood should not be shed by rape. Too many have suffered; I will not compound this injustice by ignoring it. The Romans must be halted."

Garian's face showed that he agreed with his queen's rationalisation and there would be no further argument.

There had been no sign of Julius. He seemed to have disappeared, never to return to her bed.

The sacking of Camulodunum was a rout; the garrison was caught unaware because of the complacency of the officer in charge who was too accustomed to the people of Britain obeying his orders meekly.

Ceridwen whooped with joy as she spotted one of the men who had ravished her and Cavatina. With Prasutagus's spear held high, she aimed at his neck and pierced his throat from nape to larynx. His blood gurgled from his mouth, as a crimson stream. The lance going through from one side to the other, had impaled its victim to a tree.

As Ceridwen went to retrieve the spear, a soldier came from behind and would have slain her had not Boudica sliced his head clean from his shoulders with her sword. The fortunate girl still attempted to repossess the spear, slipping on the gore and excrement of the dying man. She had one foot on the small of his back and the other on the ground, tugging with all her strength until her mother called to her to run. The garrison was waking up to its peril. Prasutagus's spear would have to be lost.

They fought battle after battle whilst Suetonius Paulinus's army was attacking the Druid Halls of Learning in Mona. One day word reached her that he was on the march back to Anglia.

When word came to her that the Roman army of the Second Augusta in Glevum had refused to engage in battle with her, Boudica considered the man to be either a fool for not obeying Suetonius or else a coward. One way or another, the Roman Governor would surely have his head? Anyway Augusta had bought her time to gather her armies about her and feed them before Suetonius caught up with them.

The lines of battle were drawn up; so far they had beaten the Roman army but this day Suetonius Paulinus was in command. The day would be long and hard; blood of British and Roman would mar the field.

They would need all the courage that she could inspire in them, reminding them that their fight was for all of Britain as well as their children and grandchildren. If ever they were to live as honourable humans then they must fight for their freedom now or forever bow their necks to the Roman boot. She shouted as loud as she could to make certain that all the fighters heard her. By the time she had finished her delicate singing voice was but a harsh croak.

Even without the aid of Augusta's troops, Suetonius struck them to the ground; the camp followers were in disarray and blocked any hope of escape for the main body of the Iceni army.

Boudica managed to gather a few of her closest commanders and her young daughter to her and led them by a secret path to the woods of Seven Snakes. It was as Prasutagus had foretold, a place of sanctuary.

155

Delirious and feverish, Boudica was unaware of the transition from land to the small boat which took them out to the galley that was waiting for them off shore.

The nightmare of being chased by something evil, returned. This time she had reached a place away from habitation. Ceridwen was running as swiftly as she could, but the child was exhausted. Suddenly the earth shook. Rocks from an overhanging cliff fell down, trapping Boudica; Ceridwen was not caught in the landslide.

"You must go on!" she called to her daughter. "You must not let him catch you! Run Ceridwen! The earth god will free me. I will catch up with you later. Now run!" she pleaded.

Gasping, Boudica awoke, drawing in a deep breath to help clear her mind. The dream had left her feeling weak and vulnerable. Tears seeped from under the bruised eyelids to slip over the corners of her eyes and run into her hair as she lay on her left side.

The nightmares tormented her; the devil chasing her took on the likeness of Julius. He was raging mad because she had refused to do his bidding. Boudica searched her memory for what it was that Julius wanted of her so much that it warranted her death.

Boudica sighed, hoping for a few hours respite from the torture of pain and bad dreams. Her head ached and throbbed, her teeth felt loose and she could taste blood in her mouth.

Resting her head on her left arm she hoped to find a few moments' rest, but the dryness in her mouth added to her misery. Closing her eyes she tried to think of the good days long ago before Prasutagus had died, and the chariot races they had had with other kings and chieftains. Prasutagus had given her a team of her own...

The smile lingered on her mouth as Boudica regained her senses. Ceridwen was cradling her head in her lap. She prised her battered eyes open to find that she was lying flat on a heaving deck. There was a rocking, tipping motion and she felt sick to her stomach.

"How long have I slept?" she asked through cracked, dry lips. Those few words had cost her dear. Her throat felt as if it were being scorched by a burning brand.

"Two days, Mother," Ceridwen replied. "We are alone with the savages who call themselves Romans. They killed everyone after they had ended their games with the women and we have been on the sea for one day.

"I have been told that they are taking us directly to Rome in this fast ligurian galley." Ceridwen searched her mother's eyes for signs of the delirium that had tormented her while she had been in a stupor but there was lucidity and understanding in their depths.

Ceridwen felt a deep sense of relief after the misery and terror of being alone, now that her mother was no longer so dreadfully ill. Once more she had a companion to share her hopes and fears. Ceridwen had been afraid that her mother would never wake, or else wake to find that her spirit had left her body, leaving an empty shell.

Chapter 38

"It's a pity that we did not go overland, then Druids could have staged an ambush and rescued us," Ceridwen said, as she wiped Boudica's brow with a damp rag. "I think that Suetonius wants us off his hands as speedily as this galleon will take us. The slaves are being whipped to row as fast as human strength will allow. The word among them is that we will be in Rome within days."

Ceridwen sensed that there was little hope of them ever returning to their lovely home in the town of Icenorum Venta alive but to keep Boudica from worrying she avoided this issue and tried to ease her mother's pain.

"You said that we are alone but who are the galley slaves, my child?" Boudica said. "There may be among them a Briton who will take home the truth of what has happened to us, for to be certain, these Roman savages will tell their own story." Her voice was gruff from the dry, excruciating swelling of her throat. She felt as if she had been without water for a moon's length and the searing agony in her arm was making her senses reel.

She looked at the men who were chained to the rowing benches; most of them were very dark skinned with huge muscles on their shoulders and arms. Those with a pale skin had black, bushy beards and they looked at the two prisoners with hatred. Blaming them for the floggings that they received if they missed a beat of the oarmaster's drum.

Then she noticed one man glancing furtively over his shoulder at them. He had long white hair, and deep blue eyes. Lines of suffering marred his strong handsome face as if he had been a slave for a very long time. He looked away, obviously afraid the Roman soldiers who had noted his interest in the prisoners.

He stood up and made his way to where the drinking water was kept in a bucket, and raised the ladle to his lips.

Then he took the bucket along the row of labouring slaves, offering them each a mouthful of the precious liquid.

As he approached Boudica and Ceridwen, he seemed to stumble and the water splashed their faces, both women opened their mouths to receive this blessing. The man was lashed for his clumsiness and put back to row at the bench. The brackish water tasted like honeyed wine to their parched tongues. The swelling in Boudica's throat made it almost impossible for her to swallow the liquid.

She looked up at the blue sky and drifting wisps of white cloud, and said, "The sea gods are kind to us, Ceridwen. I have heard it said that to cross from our shores and enter the Pillars of Hercules is a journey through hell." The sea rocked the galley gently. Now and then a stronger wave lifted it so that the outline of the coast of Gaul could be seen in the haze.

The night brought no relief. Cold and thirsty, the two women lay side by side in each other's arms. Boudica became aware of moisture trickling over her lips; was it yet another dream brought on by hunger and thirst, she wondered? The nectar of sweet wine seeped into her mouth. Instinctively she licked her lips and murmured her thanks to whatever guardian angel was giving them succour.

"Hush, drink and say nothing. I am not here; I cannot aid you further." A dark shape stood over her, blotting out the stars. She tried to open her eyes to see him properly, but he was gone as if he had never existed except for a small flask of wine left by her side.

Carefully she roused Ceridwen enough for the girl to sip some of the wine. "Where did it come from mother?"

"A guardian angel left it for us; now sleep my child."

Boudica, like her daughter, knew that there would be no return journey. This Andraste had foretold in her dreams. Glancing down at her ravaged arm, she could see the first signs of decay. The open sore had an angry red rim and yellow pus was forming at its centre. There was an ominous track of scarlet leading up towards her armpit.

Pain lingered in her bones giving her constant anguish, and the useless hand hung grey and lifeless. Her broken forearm should have been pulled into shape and strapped to a straight branch of wood or else cut off and the stump dipped in hot pitch to seal out the evil rot.

Death could not come soon enough for her, she thought, for Nero had no intention of letting her live; it was the manner of her fate that was yet to be decided.

Boudica remembered that during one trance of death, the goddess Andraste had visited her, and told her of the dreadful misfortune that was yet to come. Andraste had warned her years ago not to take up arms against a powerful enemy, and she had ignored that advice.

She would not die until Ceridwen was dead; and Cavatina, her beautiful elder daughter, with her dark curls and rosy cheeks, would go north to live and have a child. Her own death was not disclosed to her, which made her shiver with apprehension.

When Prasutagus's heart had stopped beating and he had died so suddenly, far from the roar of Mare Germanicum where his home of Icenorum Venta stood, he had left his kingdom to his daughters and to Nero believing that in doing so, his wife and daughters could enjoy freedom from concern about the matters of state and would benefit from such a powerful friend. The girls would inherit when they were of an age to be able to control the vast estates, and Boudica would not fall prey to fortune hunters.

However, as the years went by, Nero had changed from the rational, caring ruler into a despot, who bankrupted Rome with his constant building of monuments to himself.

His gigantic Golden House with its wonderful carvings and trappings had emptied the royal coffers even before the construction was finished. Hundreds of slaves toiled without rest to complete it for their master, many dying in the process.

Now Nero desperately wanted all the wealth that the Iceni had, to pay for his building programme and returned nothing except taxes, tariffs and hardship.

Chapter 39

When the Roman soldiers had abused her daughters and Boudica had been whipped like a common criminal in the market square for daring to speak out against this injustice, she had decided that it was time to throw off the yoke of oppression and brutality.

These ignorant savages even marched in their leather boots over sacred lands without pause. They had cut roads where spirits dwelt, instead of keeping to the ley lines as laid down by the gods who controlled all that was good for the people and the earth.

Her indignity at the way the Romans treated women and children, made the blood thunder in her heart. The Iceni had risen up and followed her across the country without stopping even to sow the first seeds of grain for that year's crop.

Those Druids, who had escaped the vicious assault on Mona, had guided and helped to feed her rag-tag army for many weeks.

The Iceni, Trinovatians and other tribes in accord with Boudica, had fought and won every battle against the Roman invaders, in spite of being at the mercy of the Governor General who would kill them all if he could.

Tearing the 9th Roman Legion to shreds, the Iceni army, aided by those of the neighbouring tribes of East Anglia including the Trinovatians, had rampaged through Londinium, Camulodunum and every Roman outpost along their way. They set fire to all the fine Roman buildings as they went. The streets had run with the blood of Romans and their sympathisers. Now as Boudica sat nursing her throbbing arm, chained by the ankles to a stanchion in the galleon's grey wooden deck, she realised that Suetonius was being doubly careful that she and Ceridwen could not escape the fate that the Lord Nero was planning for them!

Julius Classicus incensed Boudica. He was the son of a lady of Gaul and a high-ranking Roman officer. She had trusted him to keep secret where they would be sheltering from the Roman army if the fight went against them. Instead, he had led Suetonius, directly into the glade in which they were resting.

She was even more furious with herself and felt a deep sense of guilt for having allowed Ceridwen to come with her instead of going north to join her sister. Ceridwen had been a kind, loving and obedient child. What had this daughter of hers, whom she adored so much, done to the gods to be made to meet with the ghastly end that she sensed for her? Boudica stroked Ceridwen's hair, which had become a dull grey and matted with dirt. It no longer shone like ripe corn. "My loving child, I pray that the gods lend us a swift death, for I cannot bear to think of you in pain," she whispered and kissed the filthy mess.

"Mother, speak not of death; we may yet escape. As you say, some slaves may recognise us, and help us," Ceridwen answered, even though she too knew that the death sentence had already been passed upon them. She rejoiced in her heart that Cavatina had escaped. Word from the priests was that the rape was to bear fruit. Her body had rejected the seed sown by the men. Just as well; to have a womb full of new life, and try to fight and run would have been hopeless, and her mother would have been too concerned about her, to plan the battles.

The galley slave who had splashed their faces earlier with water, and was the probable supplier of the wine, which he had no doubt stolen, placed a bucket of seawater beside them. "Place the wounded arm in the salt water, my Lady; it will help to stop the poison from reaching the vitals," he whispered very softly, and then he picked up the now empty flask and crept away hastily.

Boudica was grateful that the slave was trying to help her, but he dared not show his concern. He had done his best. He could not set her free or save her from her fate.

She looked around at those officers who stood in the shade of a canopy to see if she could recognise anyone. Was Julius Classicus among them? Would he come to gloat?

Ceridwen lifted the injured arm for her, and gently eased it into the bucket, rinsing the cool water over the infected wound. The pain was almost more than Boudica could withstand as it shot up her arm and seemed to linger for an eternity deep in her soul. The shattered bone was thrust out and could not be replaced into the lifeless wrist.

Ceridwen could feel the tears of grief rolling down through the grime on her face. She loved her mother dearly and Boudica in turn had loved all her family deeply, her, Cavatina and her father with a love that placed them even before herself.

Bathing her mother's arm Ceridwen remembered an occasion when she had been fishing along the seashore and was cut off by the treacherous tide. Her mother had risked her life and waded through the rushing water. Boudica had carried her like a baby in her arms to safety. Seconds later the swirling tide had covered all trace of where they had been.

She tried to wipe the tears away before her mother noticed, but Boudica dried them from her cheek for her and told her, "Whatever happens to us, remember that we have known and cherished each other and we have been fortunate to have known Prasutagus and Cavatina. Indeed we have been well blessed by the gods." Looking deep into Ceridwen's eyes, she continued, " Keep the memory of them in your heart when the night is darkest." Then as she spoke, the icy fingers of insensibility crept once more into her brain.

She dreamed of long lost days of playing with her children, the friends she had made in the Druid circle, of Gildelma, who had become a firm friend and mentor. She had taught Boudica about Andraste, the earth goddess, who cared for all females because they produced the next generation, just as seed sown in the earth, the womb of Andraste, produced a harvest for the hard days of winter.

"The men may sow the seed, but it is we females who bring forth the young." Gildelma had once told her. "Without women, there would not be man, and any man with any intelligence, knows this and protects and cares for us." Gildelma had also taught her to project her spirit into the future so that she in turn could protect her Iceni tribe and tell of evil that was to come.

The warning had come from the goddess too, but in her rage, Boudica had chosen to ignore it. This slight to Andraste, and lack of prudence on her part, were going to cost her dear, of that Boudica was certain, but what else was she to do? Was she to accept these insults and brutality to her people without a murmur? I think not, she decided.

Days came and went as the ligurian, especially sent to carry the prisoners, swiftly made its way towards Rome. It was a very sturdy boat, broad of beam and deeply hulled. It could survive the worst weather that the Middle Sea could throw at it and had frequently made journeys down the coast of Africa in search of fresh slaves, gold, precious jewels, spices and valuable hard wood. The ligurian boat had been designed when it was realised that the quinquereme was too fragile and ungainly to stand up to many onslaughts in battle.

Because of the privations of the journey, flesh fell from the bones of Boudica and Ceridwen. The chains that had once been tight, hung slackly from their ankles and waists.

The poison threaded its fiery way up Boudica's arm. And no Roman came near them for fear that the she-devil would curse them. The guards had heard how Boudica had attacked Governor Suetonius Paulinus and later his throat and face had been covered with a mass of boils.

165

By the time the ship arrived in Rome, Boudica and Ceridwen were a pitiful sight, and though hunger had ravaged her strength, Boudica had taken Ceridwen by the hand and led her fearlessly through the jeering crowds. The poor girl was so famished she could hardly place one foot in front of the other.

Chapter 40

Victoria became aware that the scene had shifted abruptly and wondered why. She felt that some terrible grief had overcome this restive spirit. Looking about her, she noticed that the room Boudica had been led into was well lit by oil and pitch fed torches and candles, for it was well past the midnight hour.

There were pillars of polished pink marble, the floor was of the same material with inlays of black and gold, and no expense had been spared when this marvellous hall was built. Far different from the underground cell where she and Ceridwen had been held captive. Glancing up, she realised that she was standing in front of a dais that was curtained off by a transparent filmy screen that was soon pulled aside.

A row of silent men stood glaring at her. To one side was a throne, the occupant a handsome man who was fast going to fat; he sat leaning forward attentively, as if waiting for her to speak.

Boudica's demented mind wandered, taking her back to when she had been forced to watch Ceridwen fight for her life in the arena and it had sent her soul hurtling to Valhalla! Now she was to face the men responsible.

Revenge burned in her soul like a ravening beast. It was her only thought; she would get it, even with her last breath, if she could. With this vow she was able to hold her head high and stand straight, then look these corrupt men in the face.

The memory of Ceridwen who had stood at her back to help fight off the soldiers who had ambushed them, would stay with her for evermore. She would live no life without this responsibility on her conscience.

It was Ceridwen who had shown her real character, and courage; she had fought like a daughter of hers should, indeed, she was Prasutagus's daughter too and an

Iceni princess. Now it was her turn to show these beasts what true royalty and stamina meant.

Boudica looked around the great polished marble hall, with its huge round pillars of matching marble. There stood the half-breed in whom she had trusted; he was trying to hide in the shadows, just as he had attempted to in the forest glade. He stood alongside Suetonius and other Roman dignitaries, smirking. "Perhaps it would be amusing to your friends to tell them why you betrayed me, Classicus Julius?"

Julius, without thought of his dignity raged at her, "You laughed at me when you knew that it was your wealth that I was courting. You were not a rich widow; you were in fact reliant on the kindness of your daughters. You thought that entertaining! You laughed at me. Oh, how I have longed for this day and your destruction!" Julius shook with suppressed temper that was finally released. "I could have worn the helmet of Prasutagus and made you proud to be my queen!" Julius had no idea that he sounded like the snivelling coward that he was.

How small minded her would-be lover was. Prasutagus's wisdom had saved her from the ignominy of a loveless marriage to this quivering heap of rotting dung.

"Julius Classicus, think you that the crown of Prasutagus would have made you a king? You are wrong! It is *not* the crown that makes the king, but the man wearing it." Boudica was now smiling. Neither lover nor enemy could harm her now. They had lost all control over her when Cavatina had been slaughtered in the arena. The betrayal by Julius Classicus had opened her eyes to his duplicity.

There were those who thought that Prasutagus had omitted her from his will out of spite, and he had died hating her. How wrong they were. Boudica knew that there was not an ignoble drop of blood in his body. Prasutagus was not so stupid as to think that she would lie alone in the empty bed for long. She had the scalding hot blood of Vikings in her. A cold bed was not for her and Prasutagus was more than glad of this! Her smile was an enigma to those who watched the light and shadows cross her face.

"Prasutagus was a very shrewd man, far more understanding than you will ever be Julius. By cutting me from his will, scavengers like you would be thwarted and I would not suffer the unhappiness of a marriage that was without true affection. I wonder what woman will wish to be your lover now, knowing that you are a gold grubbing trickster?" Boudica's ugly grin gave him a premonition that he was indeed lost to love and honour. Julius' chagrin knew no bounds. His face had taken on a paler hue and eyes held a flicker of fear. The witch queen of the Iceni was right. Never would he be able to hold his head high in elevated company. He was doomed to either hide away in his native Gaul or seek forgiveness among the people that he had betrayed.

Boudica looked about the large hall. She could see no scribe to take down the happenings of the meeting of the Senate, yet he should have been there. Was he absent or was he hidden out of sight, he wondered? Why was there so much secrecy?

Turning her head slightly, she glanced around at the rest of those gathered to lay oath to her demise and noticed that it was her arch-enemy, Nero, who sat on the throne, his face impassive.

Once he had been a kind, caring man who took great pride in his just and compassionate ruling. She tried to reason with him, but he had become illogical and his stupidity knew no bounds.

A round table, upon which stood a single glass of pale green liquid, was placed between Nero and her. He started talking to her in a persuasive voice.

"It is a kindness that I offer you. The people want me to have you flogged and dragged through the streets in chains. Then you too will be a spectacle in the arena, as was your child." Nero did not add that the Senate had advised him not to commit the same mistake as Claudius, and have her crucified, making her a martyr like that Nazarene.

The taunt had sparked an even deeper resolve in her to get even with these barbarians. "My Lord Nero, the magnificent Golden Palace that you have built to ensure your popularity and as a memorial to your ego, will not last for ever. Your successors will lay waste these marvels that you have accumulated. The rooms will be filled with midden." Boudica's death mask grinned at him as she continued, "The fabulous statues that you have taken possession of will go to adorn the monument dedicated to your heirs. And those splendid buildings that you dream of building as a memorial to your greatness will be forgotten, until the truth of what has happened to my child and me, Boudica the warrior Queen of the Iceni!" The grimace stretched the dry taunt skin on her lips, making a mockery of mirth.

"Beware Nero! You follow me sooner than you expect!"

Boudica's haughty stare made Nero's stomach tremble as he gasped for breath. He leaned further forward, his gross paunch against the table with what he must have thought was a friendly smile. To her it was the grimace of death's head.

Her numb brain was telling her something, if only she could concentrate, get the pains of her abused body out of her mind. Looking down, she noticed that her ankles had been manacled again since arriving from the prison, her legs bruised and bleeding from the cruel spike driven into them to hold the manacle.

Even though I am in chains, Nero is ridiculing and baiting me, attempting to get me to take the poison. Why are they so anxious to get me to take the hemlock bane of my own free will? Why are they afraid of me, she wondered?

Slowly she prayed with her spirit to Andraste, asking forgiveness for ignoring her warning and taking her tribe to war against these inhuman Romans. And she begged the earth goddess for enlightenment. Her fogged brain steadily cleared and her suffering diminished as it brought realisation to her.

Chapter 41

It was a many years ago since Claudius had signed the death warrant for that Nazarene. No one had forgotten, and look what had happened. The people of Galilee had started to worship Him as a saviour and redeemer. He had become a victim with followers everywhere. Was He the brilliant student that Prasutagus had told her about on their wedding day all those long years ago, she wondered?

Nero would surely not want another such disturbance within the Roman Empire. Silently she thanked Andraste and the Nazarene's God for sending Jesus. His dreadful death on the cross was proving very useful. So Nero wants me to take my own life, by poison too, so that these fools can testify that I did it by my own hand, that Nero did not murder me. How little he and his half-breed informer know, she mused, controlling the urge to grin.

She was not only a queen; she had been taught by the Druids and Gildelma to be adept in the ways of the earth goddess, of prophecy and discerning the spirits who guide and protect. This would be one insult that Andraste would never forgive. For them, this life and every life they lived in the future would always end in shame and dishonour.

These men in their ignorance would force her to drink hemlock, not realising that they were condemning themselves and all they stood for to destruction if they buried her poisoned body in the earth. Andraste would not accept such an offensive offering without retaliation. She would wreak her vengeance on them, and so my Iceni family and I will be avenged. Briefly, Boudica's wandering mind had taken her thoughts away from the agony of her tortured body.

The trapped glee she felt gurgled in her throat, but what of the price that Andraste would ask from her for such an affront? I'll take whatever retribution is imposed on me, gladly, she pledged.

The everlasting rest of peace would never be hers. She too would pay with lifetime after lifetime for this ignominy. Torture and misfortune would mar her future existences. It would be worth every moment of hardship just to repay her debt of love to Ceridwen.

Her own suffering was as nothing compared to having watch her beloved daughter butchered by the animals. It was something that she would carry in her heart forever.

What she had to do was convince them that if they threw her remains to the dogs, as they probably intended, they might leave traces of their infamy, and that to remove all evidence of her having been in Rome, they would have to bury her deep, very deep.

Boudica stepped closer to the table and took the glass in her left hand. The men, anxious that she should drink, leaned toward her. Raising the hemlock in mock salute to Nero, she toasted him, "I salute you Lord Nero, and all those who have conspired against me for it is not I whom you should fear, but those who might find my wrecked body among the refuse left by the scavenging dogs outside the city walls of Rome. For even in Rome, Nero," she said in a loud clear voice, with her head held high and gazing in triumph into the emperor's fearful eyes.

Then Boudica's face contorted. There was no delight in her ominous, bruised rimmed eyes that were sunk deep in her skull, only loathing and contempt.

"I, too, have my followers as had Jesus of Nazareth. You must find a hiding place deep enough, where no one will ever find traces of your treachery." Pausing to gain breath she continued, "I die this day of poison prescribed by you," she said, pointing the jade green venom in its phial directly at him. "You too will commit suicide but not by poison, for by that time you will know what you do is wrong. You will die alone and friendless. These people whom you have summoned to attend and witness my death thereby clearing you of the sin of regicide, will desert you in your time of need."

With her face in shadow cast by the flickering torch flames, she put the clear glass with its green contents to her lips and drank the poison to the very dregs.

As the numbness crept through her limbs, and her strength gradually diminished, a sensation of nausea made her feel as if she could vomit, but her stomach had been empty of food and moisture for too long. The hemlock was absorbed as the first nourishment it had received for many days, and stayed in her body to work its evil.

The nausea and weakness persisted and she found herself on her knees, supported by her left arm. Greyness crept over her vision; her breath no longer came easily. It rattled in her throat. The grey fog, similar to that which she had encountered on her first arrival in Britain, overcast the scene about the great hall in which she had been brought by the guards, but this mist would not fade into glorious sunlight, rather it darkened into night and Boudica permitted herself to relax and accept death.

Her final moments were tormented by devils that made her skin itch unbearably. To scratch would have been bliss but there was no strength or time left to her, and just as the cock crowed to herald the coming dawn, Boudica, Queen of the Iceni, died, in the great hall with its round columns of pink marble in the Senate, in Rome. No scribe was there to note her passing and those of the Senate present, had been sworn to secrecy.

Boudica had taken on Rome, and in her death, she would destroy it.

Nero turned to the young half-caste Julius Classicus and asked him, "Do you believe that she is capable of foretelling the future and does she have friends in Rome? We forbade all Britons, except slaves, to the city of Rome. And why do you think she warned us against feeding her carcass to the dogs?" Nero was babbling and knew it, but could not stop himself.

"My Lord," Julius replied, "I personally inspected all trade and people from Britain. Only our own merchants were permitted to travel, for I too did not wish to be confronted by these angry Iceni and their Druid priests. As for the dogs, perhaps she had a fear of them? But dogs would not eat the corpse of a poison suicide. They know instinctively that they would be sick and die."

Julius breathed slowly to steady his thoughts and words, and then he continued, "And as for being able to divine the future, I have heard many tales about Boudica and her Druid friends. It is rumoured that they sacrifice anyone who is not of their faith to their gods in return for important information and good harvests." The young man knew that his own life was in danger. Nero could no longer be relied upon to forgive anyone who made mistakes.

"Her gods did not advise her well this time. Perhaps she should have offered her own daughter in exchange for her safety," Nero muttered to himself.

Julius, hoping to save his own skin, suggested that Boudica's body be thrown down the deepest well that has run dry then filled in and covered with large rocks. "There are several, high in the hills around Rome," he added.

Nero raised an inquiring eyebrow at him. "Yes, that would solve the problem. See to it!" Then he motioned for everyone to leave except Burrus, the one Guard in the palace whom he trusted implicitly.

As the paralysing effect of the hemlock had numbed the excruciating pain in her wounded arm, Boudica was able to think rationally. She cast her mind about. It was time for her to confront Prasutagus again. Frequently he had left her to go on journeys to lands beyond the sea. He had brought her and their two daughters back exquisite dresses of the finest Egyptian cotton, jewels, the like of

175

which she had never seen but he had also left her feeling empty and unloved.

Julius had made advances of love to her and for a while she had returned them. It was only the knowledge that she would be betraying her children that finally made certain that no seed of Julius Classicus would take root in her womb.

Conceivably, if Prasutagus had made her his heir, none of this would have happened. Perhaps there would have been no yoke of oppression under the heel of the Romans, and there would not have been this war.

Though yet again, Boudica considered, she would have made a complete fool of herself and trusted Julius Classicus with the Iceni kingdom. That would have been an even greater folly! Meeting Prasutagus in the next world, she would ask questions that he might find difficult to answer…that, would be interesting…

First her toes and fingers began to feel dead, then her ankles and knees as she buckled forward and slumped to the polished, ornate pink marble floor. Eventually showing no sign of vitality, her eyes closed for the last time in life. The Warrior Queen was content. She would have liked to have the same funeral rites given to other kings and queens. She was after all an Iceni Queen and the daughter of a Norse nobleman.

Chapter 42

Nero, in his ignorance would do exactly as she wanted though. Her spirit was already in Valhalla. Its resemblance to her childhood home was an enigma. Never did she dream that she would be permitted to enjoy such happiness again.

Everything was how it had been so many years ago when she was a child. The ache of bitterness in her heart melted as she went to greet Ceridwen and Prasutagus, and now, coming to greet her were her parents, and behind them were snow-topped mountains and lakes of pure azure.

Boudica's joy vanished just as she began to go towards them. She felt the tug of cord that seemed to be attached to her body, and once more she was back in that detestable room with her enemies. She felt no pain. Even her heartache at the sight of Ceridwen's torturous death, no longer hurt. She had seen her daughter's happiness at being joined with her father. Boudica waited and watched to discover why the gods had sent her back to the earth realm.

Nero called to Afranias Burrus, his most trusted guard, who stood at his back. Burrus was very short and almost as broad as he was tall. Even his face was like a roseate, round melon. "Burrus, I have a favour to ask you."

"Yes Lord, anything you wish, I will do."

"The half-breed. What do you make of him?"

"My Lord, he is a man of great ambition, greedy for wealth. Yet he could serve you well. Suetonius Paulinus is old and can no longer be trusted to make prudent decisions. The Iceni queen should not have had her arm broken like a common felon. It would have been better for her and Rome if she had apparently died in battle!" Burrus looked about the Senate meeting hall, making certain that there were no long ears about.

"You need a Pro-Consul to take command of the forces in Anglia. I can think of no better man. Classicus knows the territory and the temper of its people. It might be the chance to rid Rome of him and keep his mind off the throne of the emperor!"

Nero's bitter smile hardly reached his eyes. "Of course you are right. Burrus. Classicus can return to the land that he betrayed in honour of Rome as Pro-Consul. He can calm these irate people and perhaps we will reap some of their wealth yet." Nero paused as he considered his next move. "This bundle of bones, get Classicus to show you where the deepest pit that he knows and bury the remains of Boudica, deep!"

"At your command, my Lord." Burrus had taken an instant dislike to the half-breed. He had not fooled Burrus for a moment with the handsome and even contours of his face. The hard, ruthless mouth had reminded him of nothing else but a snake, and Burrus hated snakes.

Nero, deep in thought, heaved himself up from his throne. He did not even glance at Boudica's corpse, leaving Afranias Burrus to do his bidding. Boudica had fallen on her face. Burrus knelt down and turned her over. She looked like a heap of dirty rags rather than a noble queen. Her hip and pelvic bones made mountains in the filthy cloth. Her loins and stomach had wasted away. The putrid arm with its trail of destruction leading toward her heart, gave off a terrible stench!

But the most striking characteristic, even in death, was the laughter that played over her gaunt features. Burrus had watched many people die. He was also responsible for many deaths and had thought little or nothing of it, yet this bundle of skin and bones frightened him. He felt that she had taken a secret to the grave with her and whatever it was, it would be the end of the world, as he knew it. He called to the waiting slave to fetch a silken carpet that had come from a land far away at the end of a road that led forever eastward.

Gingerly, he placed the remains of the Warrior Queen on the carpet and gently rolled it up. Then he picked the wrapped bundle up and carried it as if it were a newborn child, outside the great palace where he placed it on the waiting chariot. Burrus sent the slave to bring Julius.

The night was cool and moonless as Burrus and Julius drove the racing chariot through the empty streets of Rome and out into the open countryside where the paved streets gave way to deeply rutted roads. Burrus held the reins with a skilled hand and rode the chariot like a seasoned mariner riding out a storm, while Julius held on with whitened knuckles as they galloped high into the lonely hills. Riding with Burrus was even more frightening for Julius than having to travel the stormy seas off the coast of Gaul. He directed Burrus to a deep ravine where the road was littered with fallen rocks.

The well was hardly discernible in the inky darkness, with rubble littered around it. The protecting surrounding wall had collapsed and there were no means of lowering a bucket or retrieving one. The shepherds who had once used it to water their flocks, had disappeared long ago when the spring that fed it dried up and the grass shrivelled and died.

The friendless wind moaned a forsaken dirge, and picked up little puffs of grit as it wandered down the barren hillside, swirling the dust around in a frenzy, only to deposit its burden once again until it became bored with playing this lonely game.

"Come, let's look at this well of yours!" Burrus said as he leapt from the chariot.

Julius stepped down gingerly; the hairs on the back of his neck standing on end. Fear gripped his stomach making him feel the need to urinate as he walked toward Burrus. His feet faltered on the loose shale and his heart beat a painful staccato against his ribs.

Julius wiped the dust laden sweat from his brow with his white cloak, knowing that there was no escape from the fate that had pursued him since he had first met the proud, haughty Queen of the Iceni. He had wanted to possess her land and wealth as well as her body and soul but she had found his need to have power over her and the Iceni too much to tolerate and when she rebelled against Rome he had decided that to gain his own ends, he must betray her whereabouts to Suetonius Paulinus. That way he would be given credit for his aid in her capture and be given a high place of duty in Nero's government. Perhaps even to be controller of Britain!

There were times when he thought that he had really won Boudica's favour after Prasutagus had joined his gods and for a while he was ecstatic. She was a warm and loving woman.

Once when he had been travelling to the northern border he had turned to watch as Boudica rode around the Iceni lands. He had seen a she wolf stand in her path. She had stepped down, spoken to the animal as if it were human, and it had lowered its head and walked back into the forest, as if Boudica were its queen too. It seemed to Julius that she held sway over man and beast.

Julius could feel fear creep into his bones. He felt that Burrus did not wish him well and he would have to watch his back for a sharp blade, just as Marius should have taken care not to take his eyes from *him*, when he had sent his soul to his gods.

Boudica had been witness to Marius's murder. She had asked why. Classicus had been mortified that it was known he could kill for self-indulgence. He wanted Boudica for himself and not have any other man block his path to the Iceni throne. Therefore Marius had to die!

Chapter 43

Burrus pushed past Julius to reach the body of Boudica. Lifting her remains from the chariot in its silken shroud, he held her to his bosom as if he were taking a dear comrade to his grave. He held her corpse over the gaping hole, then and let it fall, asking his god Jupiter to take her to his heart as a brave and vanquished warrior.

Burrus then wiped his sweating hands on his deep blue kilt and proceeded to carry out his master's wishes of filling in the well and blocking the ravine with boulders so that no one would ever discover Boudica's last resting place. He took great care to cover up all traces of disturbance on the ground to ensure that no one would ever bother her sleeping in the earth there.

Julius Classicus looked on at Burrus's hard work. Watching him heave the great stones into place, he noted that Burrus's shoulders were as broad as a bull's. His thick legs and arms made light work of picking up and moving even the largest of the rocks.

The spirit of Boudica lingered by the dried up well. She saw Julius Classicus take no part in her entombment. Most likely he did not wish to soil his hands with dirty work, but would the hands of Julius ever be free of her blood? How many lifetimes would he need to live before he forgave himself, and would he take any opportunity to mend this wrong in some way? Perhaps he would one day confess to his misdemeanour and reveal the truth of her betrayal and speak of the dreadful end to Cavatina and she, for it is not a known fact that truth will always prevail?

Boudica thanked Andraste for allowing her to see the final outcome of the exploits between herself and the might of Rome. She understood that Burrus was a soldier obeying his master but he had also treated her corpse with respect.

I'll bear you no ill will Burrus and I pray that you have some happy new lives.

Boudica would have liked to linger longer in this valley of desolation. She had become aware that for the first time, for one moon, that she had been without pain...though body pain was as nothing compared with the pain that she had felt when her baby girl had been sacrificed to Nero's animals in the arena.

Her limbs moved without the dreadful ache that had haunted her waking moments when her earthly body still clothed her spirit. She could see clearly too, even though once again it was a moonless night as it had been that fateful night when Julius had betrayed her when she and her closest followers had taken shelter in the ancient sacred oak grove.

In her heart she wanted to weep at all her mistakes. Was there no way for her to make amends and put things right?

No doubt the Roman version of what had occurred over the period since Prasutagus's death, until she herself had been coerced into drinking the hemlock, would be a story remote from the truth.

One way or another, the truth would be told though whether it was by Julius Classicus or some other witness to her demise, she did not know. Until that day, she would not rest in peace in the next world or any other world into which she was to be born!

The dust devils once more played with the debris, shifting and soughing like a tormented spirit. The loneliness of the barren hill was broken by the arrival of a black crow that perched on a rocky outcrop. Morrigu the Great Queen of the Spirit World had come for her. The Valkyrie maidens in their bright, shining armour were singing to her to come away. Odin the king of the gods, had called for her soul to join him.

182

There was Brunhild, the leader of the Valkyries, beckoning to her follow, for now she must leave behind all the anxiety of this world to be born in the next, for such was the wheel of life. These were her last thoughts on the earthly domain.

Suddenly Victoria found herself back on the empty road in the middle of the Fens. Bewildered, she stamped her feet to confirm that it was solid ground that she was standing on. Only a second ago, she had been floating beside Burrus near the well in the desolate mountains of Rome, or so it seemed.

The phantom of Boudica still stood a few feet away from Victoria. There was still the pleading expression on her face, yet the heartache that Victoria had sensed coming from the tormented spirit had now softened. It seemed wise to know that she would do everything and anything in her power to help. She tried to rationalise what Boudica required of her.

She thought that the Druid priests and friends had always been blamed for giving Boudica the hemlock, making it seem as though she had taken a coward's way out not to suffer death in the arena, but it was Nero himself who had arranged it.

Hemlock was a Roman way of suicide. Once Boudica had been captured, never would a Druid or any sympathiser of the insurrection be permitted to get anywhere near her. If Boudica, a Druid High Priestess, had wanted to take her own life, she would have used a sword or any sharp instrument to offer her blood to the earth goddess, Victoria reasoned. "You want me to put the records straight? If I try to tell the world that I met Boudica in the middle of the Fens, I'll end up certified," she murmured.

Victoria knew that she had to do what was requested of her, but how? She had no way with words. Shakespeare she most certainly wasn't! Then she asked, "Why me?

Why did you stop and ask me, after nearly two thousand years?" But the apparition was raising her good arm in farewell and fading to disappear, becoming part of the twisting and eddying fog. Victoria had never felt lonelier, even bereft.

How could that be, Victoria asked herself? The noble Queen Boudica had perished nearly two thousand years ago. She had only two daughters, and one of those she had watched die. The other one, no one on this earth knows what happened to her. She was supposed to have escaped. Did she go north, say to Lincolnshire, and have a child? The wild thoughts were chasing each other through Victoria's brain.

A wry smile touched her face as she remembered the hearsay in the family that old great-grandfather Hedges was supposed to have journeyed from Lincolnshire to Kent, leaving a worthless farm behind because of the potato famine.

There had been such a feeling of familiarity and understanding between Boudica and herself, could it be that there was a remote possibility that I have that brave woman's blood in my veins? " Nah!" Victoria chided herself. "Come back into the real world Victoria," she said almost aloud.

Standing still for a few moments longer to give her brain a chance to adjust to her normal surroundings, Victoria took a deep breath and shook her head. She still had doubts as to what had really happened.

The night air had cleared of fog and she could see the empty road stretching away endlessly into the dark. Finally, with a sigh of relief, Victoria got into her little car and turned the ignition key. Thankfully the engine fired immediately even though the lights had been left on for... how long? She looked at her watch it was still only 3am, less than two hours since she had left the party. It had seemed like days that she had been with Boudica.

The Mini purred happily along as if it were an expensive sports car and seemed to float over the bumps and potholes in the road

Eventually the long Fen road came to a junction, where Victoria saw Spalding and Terrington St Clement on the ancient, grey wooden signboard pointing to her left. To the right was King's Lynn.

"I must be half way to Lincoln," she whispered to herself. "Julia will never believe I got lost or what happened to me. Neither will the rest of world if I present this as fact." She was speaking her thoughts aloud.

King's Lynn bypass was all but empty of traffic as she navigated the numerous roundabouts. Home and a hot bath were uppermost in Victoria's mind. But the experience on the Fen road haunted her.

She put a kettle on the hob to boil while she bathed, then made a cup of tea and sat up in bed to drink it while she mulled over what had occurred.

What was it she had seen? Was it really the ghost of Queen Boudica? And why had it appeared to her? And why did the Warrior Queen trust her to tell the world the truth? There was so much to think about.

Was Prasutagus referring to Christ as the enlightened young man at Mona at the same time as himself?

It would coincide with that time in history with the fact that He disappeared for twenty years and Druid training took twenty years from the tender age of twelve until He was thirty-two with no reported sighting of Him.

On strict orders from Nero, who was afraid of *another* would be usurper, Suetonius would most certainly have destroyed all evidence of Christ's attendance at Mona.

Coincidence or not, it's certainly strange.

And it would seem that far from being fighters and warriors, the Druids were the physicians, scholars and teachers of law and order. If they had been fighters and Mona a garrison stronghold, the Romans would have met with them as soon as they landed on British soil a hundred years previously. Failing that, they would have fought Suetonius and probably destroyed his army when they attacked their home of Mona, just as Boudica had shattered the Romans living in Britain.

Victoria considered Boudica's confrontation with Nero. Had there been a scribe at her death? If so then somewhere they may still be a record. The temple of Jupiter had become Saint Peter's once Rome became Christian and all the secrets of the Roman activities were now hidden in the Vatican. Could there possibly be a manuscript gathering dust for nearly two thousand years that tells the truth? As she made ready for her bath, her brain refused to let the mystery go away.

While Victoria had been at the party, she had tied her hair up into a French pleat. Now as she waited for the kettle to boil and the bath to fill, she took out the pins that had held it so tightly. Down cascaded a waist length cape of soft golden curls with over lights of bronze. The heavy tresses framed her oval face of blush rose and alabaster white. The large grey-blue eyes were childlike in their clarity.

The hot bath steamed the mirror, and Victoria was completely unaware that she looked to a great extent like the apparition that she had met on the way home.

Eventually sitting up in bed, she raised her cup to drink the hot, soothing liquid, and as she did so, the right sleeve of her dressing-gown fell back, revealing her bare white fore arm where the livid, purple birth mark stained her flesh in exactly the same spot where Boudica's bones had been fractured.

EPILOGUE

Julius Classicus became pro consul of Britain after the death of Boudica. He replaced Paulinus Suetonius, who was considered too old and had cost Nero the wealth of the Icine nation. Julius Classicus was spying on Prasutagus, the rich and powerful king of Icine, when he saw the new queen, Boudica.

Julius Classicus was with Paulinus Suetonius when he stormed the Druid settlement at Mona and had witnessed Suetonius' brutality, however I believe that Julius Classicus would expect Suetonius to honour the unwritten law of not harming a monarch and never anticipated him to break Boudica's right arm like a common felon. Suetonius should have escorted Boudica to Rome, where Nero would treat her like royalty.

Since the first publication of this book, archaeologists in East Anglia have found many of the items written about. The gold helmet of Prasutagus and the great long spear have been found, also hoard of gold coins was found near the site named as a Roman fort at Caister, more probably the home of Prasutagus.

The great spear carried by Prasutagus was reputed to have belonged to Lugh, an Irish deity represented in mythological texts as a hero and High King. The festival Lugh began, of Lughnasadh, celebrates the harvest in August and remains one of the eight neopagan sabats.

In considering the possibility of Christ being educated by the Druids do bear in mind that He disappeared for twenty years, the length of time for a Druid learning, also the erudite thinker, William Blake posed the same question, 'And did those feet in ancient times, walk upon England's mountains green?'

Joyce Doré

Printed in the United States
142800LV00002B/17/A